"You're accusing me of hypocrisy?"

Amanda was so angry she could hardly control the shaking in her voice. "You think I'm just trying to impress other people."

Brock's dark eyes were calm as he looked around the cold, abstract apartment she called home. "Yeah," he drawled. "I think you've decorated this place for effect. I can't believe it's your own taste."

"Oh, really. We exchanged a few words at a party and that makes you an expert on me?"

"No, it doesn't," Brock said quietly. "But the minute I met you, I thought you were the most beautiful woman I'd ever seen. I also thought there was more to you than a few inches of style and glamour. After all, how could I have been wrong for all those years?"

"What do you mean, 'all those years'?"

"Forget it," Brock said abruptly. He drained his glass. "I meant something else. Thanks for a nice evening. I won't be bothering you again."

Special thanks and acknowledgment to Margot Dalton for her contribution to the Crystal Creek series.

Special thanks and acknowledgment to Sutton Press Inc. for its contribution to the concept for the Crystal Creek series.

ISBN 0-373-82523-4

NEW WAY TO FLY

New Way To Fly

Margot Dalton

Harlequin Books

TORONTO • NEW YORK • LONDON
AMSTERDAM • PARIS • SYDNEY • HAMBURG
STOCKHOLM • ATHENS • TOKYO • MILAN
MADRID • WARSAW • BUDAPEST • AUCKLAND

Dear Reader,

"Harlequin's new special series, called Crystal Creek, wonderfully evokes the hot days and steamy nights of a small Texas community... impossible to put down until the last page is turned."

—*Romantic Times*

By now, romance readers across North America have come to know and love the inhabitants of Crystal Creek. At the Double C, we've witnessed joy and sorrow and Texas grit. At the Hole in the Wall, ingenuity and surprising reunions. At the Flying Horse, there've been hard times and desperate measures. In this volume, come on out to the Double Bar, where rancher Brock Munroe is holding body and soul together... with the help of the unforgettable Alvin. Amanda Walker, shopper extraordinaire, is the last person you'd expect to transform Brock's life... or Mary Gibson's, for that matter. But Margot Dalton weaves these characters' lives together with a deft touch that will charm you, just as she did in *Cowboys and Cabernet* and *Even the Nights Are Better*.

And have you heard the news? Many readers have written to tell us that, once immersed in Crystal Creek, it's hard to leave. Well, now you don't have to! The terrific popularity of this series has prompted us to bring twelve new Crystal Creek titles your way! The series will continue with more wonderful romances created by the authors who first brought Crystal Creek to life, and authors Penny Richards and Sandy Steen will also be contributing new novels and characters to the continuing saga of Crystal Creek. Watch for them every month, wherever Harlequin books are sold.

Stick around in Crystal Creek—home of sultry Texas drawls, smooth Texas charm and tall, sexy Texans!

Marsha Zinberg
Coordinator, Crystal Creek

A Note from the Author

One of the most appealing things about Texas people is their deep love for their animals, all the way from horses to house pets. I even noticed that sentiment creeping into my books on a number of occasions, including some where the animals almost take over the story (in much the same way that Texas animals rule the hearts and households of their owners). And for those of you who may wonder after reading this book, Alvin isn't my dog. He's actually a composite of many, many dogs I've met in my life. In fact, I wouldn't be at all surprised if you see a bit of *your* dog in him!

Margot Dalton

Cast of Characters

AT THE DOUBLE BAR

Brock Munroe — Owner and sole occupant. He's running the place single-handedly.

Alvin — Brock's confidante. A mostly Australian blue heeler with a dash of terrier.

AT THE FLYING HORSE

Mary Gibson — She's coping the best she can while Bubba's doing time.

Amanda Walker — Mary's friend and the woman of Brock Munroe's dreams.

AT THE DOUBLE C RANCH

John Travis (J.T.) McKinney — Rancher, owner of the Double C, his family's ranch. A man who knows his own mind.

Cynthia Page McKinney — J.T.'s wife. An ex-Bostonian bank executive learning to do things the Texas way.

Tyler McKinney — J.T.'s eldest son, a graduate of Rice University. Now he wants to grow grapes in his daddy's pasture.

Cal McKinney — J.T.'s second son, an irresistible and irrepressible rodeo cowboy.

Serena Davis — The boot maker who's turned Cal's head.

Lynn McKinney — J.T.'s only daughter. She bucks the trend by raising Thoroughbreds in quarter-horse country.

Hank Travis — J.T.'s ancient grandfather. Old Hank has seen and done it all.

Ruth Holden — Californian vintner, and Tyler's fiancée.

CHAPTER ONE

RICH AUTUMN SUNLIGHT spilled over the hills and valleys of Central Texas, dancing on the slow-moving river and touching the rolling acres with gentle fingers of gold. The noonday sky was high and endless, the air as crisp and clear as champagne. Far overhead, a red-tailed hawk rode the soft wind currents, rising and wheeling with effortless grace.

In a small corral pen of weathered split logs, a man straightened, wiped his hot face with his forearm and glanced up at the circling hawk.

"See that?" he muttered to the animal that lay trussed and heaving on the ground in front of him. "They're lookin' for you, pal. Another few days and you'd have been breakfast for those guys."

The calf rolled his eyes and bellowed in agony. He was a large Brangus bull calf, destined someday to be a heavy thundering monster of an animal. At present, though, he was still plump and blocky, with an appealing baby look to his big dark eyes and a short blunt nose that bristled cruelly with porcupine quills.

The black-tipped quills protruded at all angles, giving the calf's head the comical appearance of a big furry pincushion. But there was nothing funny about the anguish in his dark liquid eyes, or the strangled bellows of pain that issued regularly from his mouth.

"Pore little fella," Brock Munroe muttered, gazing down at the calf, pliers dangling from his hand. He squinted up at the hawk again, then leaned against the corral rail to rest for a moment before returning to his unpleasant task.

He was a tall broad-shouldered man in his mid-thirties with a lean hard-muscled body, a handsome tanned face and a head of crisp springing dark hair that glinted warmly in the midday sunlight. A worn plaid work shirt rested easily on his wide shoulders, the seams bleached almost white by the sunlight, and faded jeans fitted snugly over his lean hips and long muscular legs.

Brock dropped to one knee beside the trembling calf to check a half hitch in the twine that held the little animal's legs knotted in position. Then, frowning with grim concentration, he clamped the pliers onto another quill.

"This won't take long now, pal," he murmured to the calf. "I already got all the bad ones. These others are loose already, an' they'll just come out like butter. See?" he added, holding a quill aloft in the metal jaws of the pliers and brandishing it before the calf's rolling dark eyes.

Brock worked doggedly, his big callused hands surprisingly gentle as he labored to extract the barbs from the calf's soft nose.

"Next time," he muttered, "you better listen to your mama, okay? I bet she told you not to mess with those porcupines. But did you listen? Oh, no. Just like all kids, had to learn the hard way, didn't you?"

His deep gentle voice seemed to have a soothing effect on the animal. Gradually the calf's trembling and straining lessened until he lay still on the dusty ground, his damp sides heaving, his neck outstretched in weary resignation.

"Now, that's the way to do it," Brock praised him, gently working out the last of the quills. "That's a real good boy. You just lie still a minute longer, an' we'll..."

He paused, reaching behind him for a bottle of yellow liquid disinfectant, which he uncapped and poured liberally over the animal's swollen bleeding nose. The calf bleated loudly in surprise and outrage, gave the big man a wild reproachful look and tried frantically to struggle to his feet.

Brock chuckled at the animal's look of pain and indignation. "That stuff smarts a bit, don't it?" he said cheerfully. "I guess I shoulda warned you."

With effortless ease, he wrestled the animal back to the ground, knelt on the calf's flank and untied the rope binding the legs. The calf kicked and rolled free, then heaved himself upright and faltered away to the other side of the corral.

Brock watched as the little animal shook his head dazedly a few times, then appeared to realize that the dreadful pain was over and the torturing barbs had vanished miraculously from his nose. Finally the calf lifted his head, bellowed joyously and trotted out through a partly open gate to the larger pen where his mother waited, lowing to her overgrown baby in soft anxious tones.

Brock grinned as he watched the reunion. His dog, Alvin, appeared at the gate and sat gazing up at the big man, tongue lolling hopefully.

"Hi, Alvin," Brock said. "You look hungry. Lunch time already?"

Alvin regarded his master with concentrated attention, one ear drooping. He was a small, engagingly ugly dog, mostly Australian blue heeler with a liberal dash of something else, possibly Scotch terrier, that gave his mottled blue-gray hide a disreputable shaggy look. Alvin's eyes were dark and perennially sad, as if the world was just a little too much for him but he was prepared to struggle bravely on.

In actual fact Alvin was a coward, especially terrified of cats and thunderstorms. He was also a lazy hedonist, dedicated to little more than his single-minded pursuit of something to eat and somewhere to sleep. He lifted his head now and looked at Brock in mournful silence, sighing heavily.

"All right, all right," Brock said, chuckling. "Just give me a minute, okay? I'll put this stuff away in the barn an' be right with you."

Apparently mollified, Alvin fell in step beside his master, plump sides twitching as he trotted along at the big man's feet.

"Pore little bull calf. He was sure hurtin' some, Alvin. Likely hasn't eaten anything for a couple days, either," Brock said to the dog, with the companionable ease of a man who spent much of his time with animals.

In fact, Brock often conversed with animals more easily than people.

Brock Munroe's values were basic and straightforward. He believed in hard work, fair play, being loyal in friendship and honest in business. He liked thick steaks, cuddly puppies and starlit nights, watercolor sunrises and gentle quiet women.

But he loved nothing in all the world as much as these five thousand rolling acres of trees and hay meadows, scrub brush and cactus, that spread out around him in the bright October afternoon sun.

The Double Bar ranch had been in the family for generations, like so many others in the Hill Country, but had fallen on hard times in recent years. Brock's father, Dave Munroe, had been a carefree, hard-living man, entirely capable of leaving his ranch at the height of calving season and driving off to some poker game he'd heard of in the next county, often straggling home days later, bedraggled and broke.

Brock's mother died when he was just twelve, leaving the boy alone with his unreliable father. And, as so often happens in such cases, Brock had grown up with a sense of responsibility far beyond his years. By the time he was sixteen he was running the big tumbledown ranch almost single-handed, and covering for his father so well that most of the neighbors didn't even suspect what was going on.

This was partly because young Brock never complained about his situation to anybody, not even his closest friends. He saw no need to complain, or to make any attempt to change his life. Brock Munroe loved his father and he loved his home. From earliest boyhood, nothing mattered to him as much as keeping the ranch together, striving against all odds to make it viable.

Old Dave Munroe had finally driven his truck off the edge of the river road one stormy night a few years ago, and after that Brock's life was lonelier but a lot less complicated.

"Yeah, he was a real ol' hummer, Dad was," Brock said to his dog, remembering how hard he'd had to struggle to pay off his father's debts. "But he sure enjoyed life while it lasted, you gotta say that much for him."

Alvin sighed in polite agreement and lingered impatiently on the doorstep, looking up with hopeful eyes at the big man beside him.

Brock grinned. "You don't give a damn about life an' death an' ultimate fulfillment, do you, Alvin? You just wanna know where your next meal's comin' from. An' more important, *when* it's comin'. Right?"

Alvin gave his master a disdainful look and pushed in front to enter the house first, his plump body swaying as he made his way through a welter of scattered paint cans, old rags, bits of sandpaper and discarded pieces of plywood.

"Gawd, what a mess," Brock muttered aloud. "Alvin, when's the work gonna settle down around here enough for me to finish all this, d'you think?"

Alvin made no reply, except to pause by his dish and squat. He stared up at Brock with passionate concentrated attention, his mouth partly open, his tail thumping gently on the worn linoleum.

Brock upended the paper sack of dog food, tipped a liberal amount into Alvin's bowl and then washed his hands thoroughly at the sink. He wandered across the room, towel in hand, to give the contents of his fridge a gloomy inspection.

"What I need," he told Alvin with a wistful note in his voice, "is a wife. You know that, Alvin? A wife would be so nice to have around."

Alvin glanced up briefly, jaws moving with rhythmic speed, dark eyes half-closed in bliss. Then he dropped his head and buried his nose once more in his dish.

Brock watched the dog for a moment, a little sadly. At last he turned, took a few slices of bread, a chunk of salami and an apple from the fridge and wandered into the living room, which was also cluttered with renovation materials.

Brock had begun the improvements to the old house earlier in the year, when he realized that, for the first time in living memory, he was actually going to have some extra money.

Still, he was doing all the work himself, learning as he went along from manuals and how-to books. Like everything Brock did, his carpentry was neat, precise and destined to last a lifetime. But the work was time-consuming and there never seemed to be enough hours in the day to complete the tasks.

Another, more serious problem was the fact that he needed advice on things like planning and color selection. For instance, Brock wasn't at all sure how to make his kitchen convenient to work in, or which colors to choose, or where to place windows to get the most light.

Sometimes Brock toyed with the idea of asking advice of a longtime friend like Lynn McKinney or Carolyn Townsend, somebody who could give him a woman's point of view. But he always shied away from the prospect, and he wasn't even sure why.

Of course he told himself it was just because the place was such a mess that he didn't want anybody to see it. But he suspected that his reluctance went deeper than that. After all, people like Lynn and Carolyn and Mary Gibson were all good friends, nice women, neighbors he'd known all his life.

The problem was, they just weren't *her.*

Brock frowned and lowered himself into his sagging old cut-velvet armchair, thinking about the shadowy woman who lived at the back of his mind.

She'd been his fantasy as long as he could remember, this lovely fragrant delicate woman with the shining dark hair and vivid blue eyes, the dainty curved body and regal lift to her head. More times than he could count, he'd seen her smiling though the clouds when he rode out to bring in the cattle before a storm, heard her laughter drifting on the autumn wind, felt the soft caress of her lips in the gentle rains of spring.

Sometimes Brock Munroe ached for his imaginary woman with an urgent desire that left him limp and breathless with longing, and a savage need that other women's bodies could never quench for long. There was just something about her that was so...

Brock shook his head restlessly.

He'd always considered this fantasy a little crazy but essentially harmless; the kind of thing that would vanish as soon as a real flesh-and-blood woman entered his life. In fact, during the years when his father had been getting harder and harder to handle, and even more recently when Brock had been struggling all alone to save the ranch from ruin, he hadn't given the matter much thought at all.

But he was thirty-five now, and he was beginning to worry sometimes, in the lonesome darkness of the night, that maybe he was never going to find a woman to satisfy him.

There was no shortage of applicants, it seemed. Any evening that he bothered to clean up and drive into town, there were plenty of women around who appeared eager to dance with Brock Munroe, to accept a drink or dinner or whatever he was in the mood to offer. But they all fell short of his elusive ideal.

Brock had begun to grow increasingly impatient with himself. He tried to accept the fact that his dream woman was a fantasy and nothing more, and that he should let her go and find somebody real to settle down with. It was time to build a life, have a couple of kids and make the old ranch a busy happy place again.

In fact, he'd almost succeeded in convincing himself that this was the wisest course of action. And then, one night just a couple of weeks ago, he'd seen her.

Not in person, of course. After all, women like that didn't tend to turn up in Claro County. He'd seen her on television, one night when a driving autumn thunderstorm was throwing noisy buckets of rain against the blackened windows, and the wind sighed mournfully around the eaves of the creaking old house.

Brock had been lounging in his sagging armchair with a book in his hands, pleasantly weary after a long day, almost nodding off with Alvin curled snugly at his stockinged feet. At first he thought the woman on the television screen was just another fantasy, a kind of half-waking dream. But when he sat up and looked more closely, he saw that it was really her, and he began to tremble wildly with excitement.

Then she was gone, vanishing as suddenly as she'd appeared, replaced by a lot of people talking about how well their new cars handled. Brock could still remember the searing disappointment, the way his hands shook and his heart pounded while he sat staring blankly at the television screen.

But she'd reappeared in the next hour, and several times after that.

Brock grinned, recalling as well how unnerved he'd felt when she came back on the screen. He'd been trembling like a puppy, almost too excited to get the segment recorded on tape. Now, remembering, he picked up the remote control for his VCR, flicked the buttons and activated a tape already on the machine. Then he took out his jackknife, settling back to cut pieces of salami and wedge them between slices of bread, chewing thoughtfully on his rough sandwiches as he gazed at the television.

There was a rush of noise, a flicker of snow and ragged colored bands, and then the image of a woman sitting quietly with folded hands in a soft velvet chair before a dark backdrop.

Although he'd watched the commercial dozens of times, Brock still caught his breath when he saw the woman. He sat and stared at her with rapt attention, his lunch forgotten in his hands.

She was so exquisite, lovely and desirable, so exactly the woman he'd visualized all these long lonely years. Her dress was plain, dark and beautifully fitted on a dainty curved body. She had wide blue eyes, an oval face with high cheekbones and a lovely warm mouth, and her skin was cream, almost translucent, in breathtaking contrast with her shining black hair.

Brock continued to gaze at the woman, studying every nuance of her voice and gestures. She had the calm assured manner and the elegant, high-born Spanish look that ran through so many prominent Texas families. In fact, Brock had always visualized his woman in white lace with that dark hair pulled straight back from her face and gathered low on the nape of her neck, and jewels in her dainty ears.

But this woman wore her hair in a short bouncy style, the kind of casual sophisticated haircut that looked simple but probably cost enough to stagger any poor working rancher. Brock didn't know if he liked the hairstyle or not, but there was still no denying that this was his dream woman, the exact face and form that had haunted him throughout his life.

Her name was Amanda Walker, she told the camera with a calm gentle smile. She was a native of Dallas, but had worked in the retail industry in New York for a number of years, and she wanted to let the world know that she had just opened her own business, a personal shopping service in Austin, Texas.

Brock settled back in his chair, wondering for the hundredth time just what a personal shopping service was. He frowned when Beverly Townsend appeared on the screen and pirouetted slowly, while his dream woman talked to the camera about the outfit that Beverly was wearing.

Brock didn't like to see his dream woman in the same setting as Beverly. In fact, he'd never had a lot of admiration for the beauty-queen looks of Beverly Townsend, although his friend Vernon Trent, who was engaged to Beverly's mother, assured him that Beverly was a much different girl these days. Apparently she'd fallen in love with a nice basic kind of guy, and set aside a lot of her airs and pretensions. Still, Beverly represented the jet-set life-style to

Brock Munroe, a type of glamour and idle sophistication that he had scant respect for.

"Notice how versatile the blazer can be," the dark-haired woman said in her sweet musical voice. "It works well with a slim skirt for the office, and equally well with chinos for the weekend, so it's really a dual-purpose investment. And the blouse, although it's quite expensive, can also be..."

Brock watched Beverly's lovely body turn slowly in front of him, but he was unmoved by her golden beauty. He had eyes only for the slim quiet woman in the chair, who was now discussing what she called "the art of accessorizing."

"A lot of women will choose a tasteful expensive outfit, and then go out and buy big plastic earrings that exactly match the color of their blouse," Amanda was saying. "That's a fatal error. Now, these small gold hoops are..."

Alvin wandered into the room, looking sated, and fell with a heavy thud onto the floor at Brock's feet, resting his chin mournfully on his front paws.

"Hey, Alvin," Brock said, waving the heel of the salami roll, "did you know that it's a fatal error to buy plastic earrings that are the exact color of your blouse?"

Alvin lifted his head and stared blankly at his master, then caught sight of the unfinished chunk of salami and gazed at it with sudden attention, his ears alert.

"You glutton," Brock said in disbelief. "You're stuffed, Alvin. You couldn't possibly want to steal the last morsel from a poor starving man."

Alvin half rose, his tail beginning to wag slowly as he continued to stare at the small piece of meat with fierce concentration.

"All right, all right," Brock muttered. "Here, let me have one last bite an' then you can take the rest."

He tossed the meat to the plump dog, who caught it in midair and chewed it with pleasure, sinking down again to worry the last mouthful in his teeth while Brock watched him gloomily.

"If you had plastic earrings that exactly matched your blouse, you'd never get to wear 'em anyhow, Alvin. You'd *eat* the damn things," Brock said, nudging the dog with his foot.

His brief interaction with his dog had caused him to miss the end of the television commercial. Brock reached for the control to rewind the tape, and was about to settle back for another viewing when his telephone rang.

"Hello?" Brock said, lifting the receiver and glaring at Alvin, who had finished the salami and was now giving speculative attention to Brock's uneaten apple on the coffee table.

"Hello to you. Is this my best man?"

"Vern!" Brock said, grinning cheerfully. "Hey, it's almost time, ol' buddy. Did the condemned man eat a hearty meal?"

"Look, Brock, I'm not getting executed, I'm getting married. I think there's some difference, you know."

"That," Brock said, "depends entirely on your point of view. What's up?"

"Just checking," Vernon said, sounding almost too happy to contain himself. "Making sure you're going to remember to bring the ring, and all that."

"Look, Vern, I like you some, but if you bother me one more time about that damn ring, the wedding's off. I won't come."

Vernon chuckled. "Come on, have a heart. It's a big day for me, Brock. I've waited forty years for this woman, you know, and I want everything to be just perfect."

"Well, you sure do sound a whole lot happier than any man has a right to be," Brock said, feeling suddenly wistful. "An' you don't have to worry, Vern. I'll bring the ring, unless Alvin eats it before I can get it to you."

"If he eats it," Vernon said in the dark tone of one who was well acquainted with Alvin's habits, "then Manny will just have to do a little emergency surgery this afternoon. You tell Alvin that, Brock."

Brock chuckled. "I'll tell him," he said, looking down at Alvin, who seemed to understand the conversation, and was eyeing his master with sudden deep apprehension.

"So, it's three o'clock at the courthouse, okay? Second floor?"

"Yeah, Vern. As if you haven't told me that about a thousand times already. I'll be there."

"Are you dressed yet?"

Brock laughed. "No, Vern, I'm not dressed yet. I just finished pulling a couple dozen porcupine quills outa one of my little Brangus bull calves, an' now I'm having my lunch."

"But...shouldn't you be getting ready by now? It's past one o'clock," the other man said.

"Vern, settle down," Brock told him gently. "Everything's gonna be just fine. There's nothing to worry about. I'll be there before three, an' I'll have the ring, an' you an' Carolyn will get married, an' then we'll all go out to the Double C for a nice big party. Nothing will go wrong. Relax, okay?"

"I guess you're right," Vernon said. "I just can't believe it's really happening, Brock. I'm so damned happy."

"Well, you deserve it, fella," Brock said gently. "An' I'm happy for both of you. I truly do wish you all the best, Vern. Now, go have a stiff drink or something, an' try to pull yourself together, an' I'll see you in a little while."

They said their goodbyes and hung up. Brock sat staring at the telephone for a long time. At last he levered himself upright, dislodging Alvin, who had fallen asleep on his master's stocking feet. He walked to his bedroom.

Unlike the rest of the house, this room was tidy, with a bright woven rag rug on the hardwood floor, a clean faded spread covering the neatly made bed and a bank of worn colorful books in handmade shelves along one wall.

Brock gazed wistfully at the books. Normally, he allowed himself a half hour or so of reading in the middle of the day, a treat that he looked forward to all morning.

But then he recalled the panicky tone in Vernon Trent's voice and shook his head.

"Poor ol' Vern," he said to Alvin, who had followed him into the room and was trying to scramble up onto the bed. "I guess I should try to be early if I can, just so he doesn't fall apart before the ceremony gets under way. Alvin, you're such a mess," he added, watching the fat dog struggle in vain to scale the high old-fashioned bed. Alvin fell back heavily onto the rug.

Brock scooped up the dog and tossed him onto the bed, grinning as Alvin gathered his dignity with an injured air, turned around briskly a few times and sank into a ragged ball in the center of the mattress, ears drooping contentedly, eyes already falling shut.

"Gawd, what a life," Brock commented enviously, watching the sleepy dog for a moment. Finally he turned, stripped off his shirt, jeans and socks, and padded down the hall to the bathroom, his hard-muscled body gleaming like fine marble in the shaded midday light.

He showered energetically, singing country songs aloud in a pleasant deep baritone, toweled himself off and then examined his face in the mirror, fingering his firm jaw.

"Better shave again," he muttered aloud. "There'll likely be somebody taking pictures, an' Carolyn's not gonna like it much if I'm showing a five-o'clock shadow in every photograph."

He lathered his face and began to shave carefully, thinking about the strange twist of fate that had brought his dream woman to appear to him on the same television screen with Beverly Townsend, the daughter of the woman that his friend Vernon Trent was marrying today.

Because, of course, Brock was fully aware that if he decided to make use of this connection, he could learn more about the mysterious woman, maybe even get to meet her.

He paused, razor in his hand, and gazed into his own dark eyes, wondering if he really wanted to meet Amanda Walker. After all, there was a certain risk to having dreams come true. The woman in his fantasies had warmed and sustained him through a lot of hard lonely years, but would the reality of her be as satisfying as his dreams?

Brock frowned, thinking about the woman in the velvet chair, recalling her air of sophisticated grace and calm elegance. That hadn't really disturbed him, because he'd always pictured his woman as being quiet, gracious and serenely poised. What did bother him was the kind of superficial ambience the television commercial exuded, the popular idea that "image was everything." And despite her serenity the woman on the television screen seemed ambitious, almost a little hard-edged.

Brock shook his head, still gazing thoughtfully at his reflection. The misted glass of the mirror shimmered before his eyes and he saw her face again, that lovely pure oval with the warm sapphire eyes and a mouth made for kissing. She was gazing at him, inviting him, lips softly parted, blue eyes full of tenderness and an alluring elusive promise so wild and sweet that his knees went weak and his body began to tremble with longing.

Then, abruptly, she vanished and Brock was staring into his own brown troubled eyes again, feeling strangely bereft.

"You're such a fool," he told himself, gripping the handle of his razor in a shaking hand. "You're such a goddamn fool."

Grimly he returned to his task, forcing himself to concentrate on the day ahead. But then he remembered the joyous tone in Vernon Trent's voice and his friend's unashamed declaration of happiness, and he felt lonelier than ever.

At last he finished shaving, rinsed off his razor and cleaned the sink mechanically, then wandered back into his bedroom to dress.

He paused in front of his closet, gazing in brooding silence at the few clothes that hung there, mostly Western-style shirts and clean folded jeans.

When Vernon had asked Brock Munroe to be his best man, he'd questioned Brock tactfully about suitable clothing for the occasion, and Brock had assured his friend that of course he had a dark suit.

And he did, but it was the same suit he'd worn to his high school graduation, almost twenty years ago. Brock lifted the suit bag from its hanger and unzipped it, examining the garment inside and wishing that he'd taken the time to buy something new for the wedding.

Brock frowned, holding the plain black suit aloft in his brown callused hands and gazing at it. He'd tried it on recently, and it still fitted reasonably well. How could anybody possibly tell that it wasn't brand-new?

"After all, I only wore the damn thing a couple times in my whole life," he said defensively to Alvin, who was watching him with sleepy detachment. "It's just like new. Why should I spend all that money on another one, just for one day?"

He thought again of Amanda Walker's television commercial, and remembered her sweet voice commenting that image perfection consisted of tiny intangibles that added up to a total look.

"Tiny intangibles!" Brock scoffed aloud to his dog, trying hard to feel as confident as he sounded. "Like what? Clean socks? No soup stains on your tie? Well, I can look after stuff like that as well as the next guy, Alvin. I'm not worried."

He dressed rapidly in the dark suit and a crisp white shirt that he'd spent almost half an hour ironing the day before. Finally he slipped on black socks and sturdy polished brogues, knotted his dark maroon tie and glanced at his watch in sudden panic.

"Look after things, okay, Alvin?" he said, heading for the door, rushing out through his cluttered kitchen and down the walk to his truck. A minute later he was back in the room.

"Forgot the damn ring," Brock said to Alvin with an abashed grin. He rummaged in a bureau drawer for a small velvet case, which he slipped into his suit pocket.

Alvin coughed and gnawed rudely on one of his hind paws.

Brock gave the ugly little dog a cold glance. "Alvin," he said, "you're a real hard dog to love, you know that?"

Then he was gone, running lightly out through the house and down to his truck.

Alvin waited a moment, listening to the fading hum of the vehicle motor down the long winding road. Then he stood, yawned and scrambled off the bed. He paused to scratch himself with great energy, then wandered out into the messy living room, checking wistfully to see if any surviving bits of the salami had somehow lodged under the chair or coffee table.

CHAPTER TWO

THE NOISY WEDDING celebration swirled through the entire lower floor of the big Double C ranch house, occasionally spilling out onto the veranda and patio. Lettie Mae Reese and Virginia Parks, cook and housekeeper respectively at the Double C, circulated among the laughing crowd carrying heaped trays of food, exchanging news and jokes with people they seemed to have known all their lives.

In fact, Amanda Walker thought wistfully, everybody here seemed to have known everybody else since birth. The merry gathering exuded family warmth and intimacy. It made her feel lonely and out of place.

Amanda knew hardly any of the people at this party except for the bride, Carolyn Townsend, her new husband, Vernon Trent, and Carolyn's daughter, Beverly, whom Amanda had met years ago at college. And of course she knew her host and hostess, J.T. and Cynthia McKinney, as well as J.T.'s adult children.

But all these other people were strangers to her, loud-talking sun-browned people with drinks in hand, laughing uproariously and hugging each other and shouting ribald jokes at the smiling couple seated near the fireplace.

Amanda stood quietly beside a curtained alcove, gazing at Vernon and Carolyn, her blue eyes misty with affection. They both looked warmly contented and so deeply in love that when they smiled at each other they seemed to have no connection to the rest of the world. They were alone in their quiet circle of tenderness.

Amanda hadn't attended the actual wedding ceremony, fearing that her presence might be an intrusion, though Beverly had pressed her to come to the courthouse with the rest of them. Now she wished she'd gone, just so she'd have a memory of these two people exchanging their vows. Vernon Trent and his new wife both seemed so completely happy, so perfect for each other.

Amanda noted as well, with a practiced professional eye, that the bride was dressed beautifully. She wore a trim silk suit of pale smoky mauve that looked wonderful with her fine tanned skin and golden coloring.

From long habit, Amanda glanced around the crowded rooms, playing the familiar game of trying to pick out the best and worst-dressed women guests at the party.

With no hesitation at all she awarded the best-dressed accolade to Cynthia McKinney, even though the woman was very pregnant. Cynthia, who had been one of Amanda's very first clients, wore a flowing, deceptively simple top of pale glimmering silver that swirled over slim black silk trousers, and she looked graceful and glamorous despite her impressive bulk.

Worst dressed was harder to decide on, Amanda told herself with a wry private smile, because there were some truly atrocious outfits scattered throughout the big room. Bulging velour jumpsuits, low-cut sweaters with rhinestone appliqués, a tight leather miniskirt and patterned panty hose...

Suddenly Amanda's critical eye fell on the worst mistake of all, a sagging polyester pantsuit of the kind she fervently wished would vanish from the face of the earth. This one was a faded rusty color with shapeless jacket, plastic buttons and a tacky fringed scarf that did nothing at all to improve the look.

The woman, whoever she was, stood sideways with her face turned away from Amanda, and her figure didn't seem nearly as terrible as her outfit. She appeared to be in her late forties or early fifties, with carelessly styled graying auburn hair and weathered skin.

Amanda was eyeing the woman with pained attention, picturing how a soft windblown haircut and some clothes that suited her wholesome fine-boned look would transform this woman. Possibly a rough slub-linen jacket in a raw oatmeal shade, and a longer soft wool skirt with a . . .

Just then the object of her attention turned to look past Amanda at somebody across the room. Amanda gazed at the older woman's face, stunned by the expression she saw there. Amanda forgot her criticism of the woman's clothes, speculations about image improvement, everything but a wrenching sympathy and a passionate desire to help.

"Having a good time all alone in the corner, Amanda? Come on, why aren't you socializing and getting to know people?"

Amanda turned to smile at her friend Beverly Townsend, who was undoubtedly one of the most beautiful and well-dressed women in the room. Beverly's blue eyes shone with excitement, and her lovely golden face was glowing.

Amanda suspected that at least part of Beverly's glow was due to the young man behind her. Jeff Harris had paused to joke with a group on the other side of the archway while Beverly tugged impatiently at Amanda's sleeve, trying to draw her friend out into the room.

Amanda shook her head. "Beverly Townsend," she teased, "this isn't a college dorm party, you know. We're both twenty-five years old. Don't you think it's about time you quit trying to line me up with eligible men?"

"Oh, pooh, I'm not talking about *men,*" Beverly protested, though the mischievous sparkle in her eyes somewhat belied her injured tone. "I'm talking about potential customers. Come on, Mandy," she whispered, leaning closer to her friend, "look at the *clothes* some of these women are wearing. Now, could they or could they not use some professional help with their image?"

Amanda nodded. "Maybe," she said, her eyes falling involuntarily on the tight leather miniskirt and black-spangled panty hose that swayed past Beverly at that moment.

"Oh, *her,*" Beverly said with scorn, following Amanda's gaze. "That's Billie Jo Dumont. Forget it, Mandy, she's hopeless. She doesn't have the sense God gave a chicken, or she wouldn't have come here at all today. It's hardly even *decent,*" Beverly added, her blue eyes suddenly fierce.

"Why not?" Amanda asked, bewildered. "I mean, it's a truly tacky outfit, but you can't really call it indecent, Bev."

"No, no, I was talking about her gall, coming to this party." Beverly leaned closer to her friend. "See the woman by the archway, that nice little lady in the awful polyester pantsuit?"

Amanda nodded, trying not to gaze conspicuously at the woman Beverly indicated.

''Well, that's Mary Gibson.'' Beverly paused for dramatic effect, giving Amanda a pointed significant glance.

Amanda looked at the other woman in puzzled silence. ''The name kind of rings a bell,'' she said at last, ''but I...''

''Bubba's wife,'' Beverly whispered. ''Bubba Gibson.''

Amanda's eyes widened. ''The one who's in jail? He killed somebody, didn't he?''

''He killed some of his horses for the insurance. If it had just been *people* he killed,'' Beverly added, ''folks around here would probably be able to forgive him. But horses, that's something else altogether. Far, far more serious.''

Amanda gazed at her friend, startled and appalled. ''You're kidding. Aren't you, Bev?''

Beverly considered. ''Maybe a little,'' she conceded, ''but not much.''

''And the girl in the leather skirt, where does she come into it?'' Amanda asked.

Beverly eyed her beautiful dark-haired friend with scant patience. ''Come on, Amanda,'' she said, sighing. ''You've been living in Austin for months, and visiting out here all the time, and it's all anybody's been talking about. How can you not know what's going on?''

Amanda shrugged. "I don't pay much attention to gossip," she said. "You know that, Bev. I'm just not that interested in dishing the dirt."

"Well, it's dirty, all right. The girl in the miniskirt, she was Bubba's mid-life folly long before the mess with the horses. That little affair went on for ages, right under Mary's nose, and everybody knew it. They were just awful, the pair of them."

Amanda's blue eyes widened. She gazed surreptitiously at the gorgeous young woman with her pouting red lips and sumptuous figure, and then at the stiff middle-aged woman in the dowdy suit who stood near the archway.

"The poor woman, Bev. How can she stand it?"

"It can't be easy," Beverly agreed with a flash of the generous compassion that often surprised people who didn't know her well. "And the worst part of it is that Mary's such a darling. She truly is, Mandy. Everybody loves her. And she's never said one word against Bubba, not once during this whole mess. If she has opinions, she keeps them to herself."

She keeps her agony to herself, too, Amanda thought. *And it's probably going to kill her, the poor woman.*

"Come with Jeff and me," Beverly was urging in an obvious attempt to change the subject. "There's lots of people I want you to meet. You can't hide here in the shadows all evening, girl."

"Hmm?" Amanda asked, giving her friend a distracted glance.

"I *said,* I want you to come with me and..."

"Oh, right. Sure, Bev, in a minute, okay? I just have to...to find a powder room, and then I'll come right out. Where will you be?"

"On the patio. Just through that door over there," Beverly said, pointing with a graceful scarlet-tipped finger. "Don't get lost."

"I won't," Amanda promised. "I'll be out right away."

She stood watching with an automatic smile as Beverly took Jeff's hand, paused to give him a quick kiss and headed for the patio, dragging the handsome young man laughing behind her.

After they were gone, Amanda took a fresh drink from one of the serving girls, exchanged a few cheerful remarks with the youngster and then edged toward the woman by the archway, who was gripping her elbows in white-knuckled hands and staring at the swirling crowd with a blank unseeing stare.

"Hello," Amanda said in her quiet musical voice. "My name's Amanda Walker."

The older woman turned to look at her with a dismal expression. Then she smiled and her face was transformed. Mary Gibson had a luminous, childlike smile that lit her weathered features and shone warmly in her hazel eyes. Amanda swallowed hard and smiled back.

"I'm Mary Gibson," the woman said, extending a slim brown hand. "And I know who you are."

"You do?"

"I saw you on TV. I think you're just beautiful."

"Oh." Amanda's cheeks tinted a delicate pink when she thought how trivial her show about correct accessorizing must seem to Mary Gibson.

But Mary didn't seem at all troubled by the superficial glamour of Amanda's presence or position.

"That one outfit," she said wistfully, "the one Beverly wore, you know, that was all white with a little trimming around the edges?"

Amanda nodded, gripping the stem of her glass and smiling absently as a couple brushed past her, shouting loudly to someone across the room.

"Well, I thought that was just the most beautiful thing I've ever seen," Mary said shyly. "And when you showed how the silver earrings highlighted it and brought out the turquoise tones, I could see exactly what you meant."

Amanda felt a quick rush of pleasure, and a surprising desire to hug the woman.

"You know, I'm so glad to hear you say that. I wasn't convinced that the image would translate all that well onto the television screen," she said.

"Watching those commercials of yours, it always makes me wish I was thirty years younger," Mary went on in the same wistful tone. "It must feel so wonderful to wear clothes like that, and look pretty in them.''

"Why would you have to be younger?'' Amanda asked. "You'd look beautiful in clothes like that right now, Mary.''

The other woman gave her a quick wary glance, as if fearful that she was being made fun of. But Amanda returned Mary Gibson's gaze quietly, her lovely face calm, her eyes warm and sincere.

At last Mary shrugged awkwardly and looked away into the crowd. "That's just plain silly,'' she said in a flat miserable voice. "I couldn't wear clothes like that. I wouldn't know the first thing about buying them, and even if I did, I couldn't afford them.''

"Buying clothes for people is my job, Mary,'' Amanda said. "That's what I do for a living. It's what the television commercials are all about. And as for the prices, well, it just so happens...''

She paused and set her wineglass on the tray of a passing server, then folded her hands behind her back and crossed her fingers childishly. Amanda always hated telling lies, even tiny little white ones, and she was about to come up with a real whopper.

But she thought about Mary Gibson's sad defeated look and the sudden childlike wonder of that glowing smile, and steeled herself to plunge on.

"It just so happens,'' Amanda said, "that I've had a bit of bad luck this past month, Mary. I bought quite a lot of things on spec for a woman who...who got sick, and has to spend a few months in therapy, and she doesn't feel like buying anything new just now. So I'm stuck with them. And the odd thing is, this woman is just about your size and coloring. I think some of them would be perfect for you."

Amanda paused for breath and found Mary Gibson staring at her with that same wary cautious look. But there was something else in the woman's eyes, too, a glint of hope and longing that nerved Amanda to continue with her story.

Not that all of it was a complete lie. The clothes she was talking about *did* exist, all right. But they were Amanda's own clothes, hanging in the bedroom closet of her apartment back in Austin.

Amanda allowed herself a brief flash of private humor, thinking how aghast her New York friends would be if they knew that Amanda was proposing, quite literally, to give this virtual stranger the clothes off her back.

But, Amanda told herself, they hadn't heard Mary Gibson's story. And they hadn't seen that small shining smile of yearning. Besides, Amanda wasn't being completely selfless. There was a plan forming at the back of her mind, a way that she might turn this generous impulse to her business advantage.

"I couldn't afford clothes like that," Mary said finally, with a brief hopeless shrug. "They'd be far too expensive for my budget. Things are real tight around my place these days."

"You might be surprised," Amanda said. "You see, I'm just starting out in business, Mary, and things are awfully tight for me, too."

At least *that* statement was the absolute truth, Amanda told herself grimly, pausing to take a praline from a tray carried by Virginia Parks.

"So, what I'd be willing to do," she went on, chewing the small sugary confection, almost overwhelmed by the delicious flavor, "is sell you a few of the outfits at cost, just to get them off my hands."

Mary hesitated. "How much would 'cost' be?" she asked after a moment.

"Well, it varies, of course. One of the outfits I'm thinking of particularly is a two-piece suit, kind of a longer Chanel style, in a really soft wool that would be just lovely on you."

Amanda paused, feeling a tug of regret at the thought of parting with this particular suit, one of her personal favorites.

"And how much would it be?" Mary asked.

"Let me see . . ." Amanda pretended to calculate. "My cost, plus shipping expenses, less dealer tax . . . I could probably let you have it for around a hundred, if you decided you liked it."

Mary's weathered face brightened. "Really? That's a pretty good deal, isn't it?"

Damn right it is, Amanda thought gloomily. *Especially since I paid more than nine hundred for it at Saks just a couple of months ago....*

But her face betrayed none of these thoughts. "I think it's a pretty good deal," she agreed quietly. "And if you liked, I could bring a few of the other pieces, too, sweaters and blouses and slacks, and you could try them on in private at home before you made a choice."

"Oh," Mary sighed. "Oh, my, that'd be so nice. You know," she added impulsively, gazing at the younger woman, "I think I really need something like this, Miss Walker. My life's been ..."

She paused and flushed awkwardly, then continued. "The way things have been happening, my life hasn't been all that good lately. And I could really use a little lift like that. Something to make me feel ... better about myself, you know?"

"I know," Amanda murmured. "I know you could, Mary. Everybody needs a lift now and then. When would you like me to bring the things over for you to try on?"

"Oh, any time, I guess. Would it be ... would you be coming fairly soon?" Mary asked wistfully.

Amanda nodded, considering the week ahead, reorganizing her schedule rapidly to accommodate another trip to Crystal Creek. If she could bring out the new winter outfits for Lynn McKinney on Wednesday, then she'd be able to...

"Miss Walker?"

Amanda smiled. "You'd better call me Amanda, if we're going to be doing business together. I was just thinking about my week, Mary. Would Wednesday be good for you? Say about two o'clock?"

Mary nodded, rummaging in her handbag. "That'd be real nice. Just let me find a pen, and I'll draw a map so you can find my place."

"No problem," Amanda said, waving her hand in dismissal. "I'll be stopping off here and over at the Circle T. Someone can give me directions when I get there."

"Oh, it's real easy," Mary said. "I'm just a few miles out on the other side of town, bordering Brock Munroe's place."

"What's this?" A cheerful male voice came from the other side of the archway, beyond Amanda's line of vision. "Mary Gibson, are you talking about me behind my back?"

Mary smiled and turned away to peer at the newcomer, who was still hidden from Amanda. "Hi, Brock," she said. "My, don't you look spiffy, all dressed up in a suit and tie."

"I feel like a trained monkey in this rig," the man with the deep voice said, reflecting such rueful distaste that Amanda smiled and leaned around the archway to see what he looked like.

At the same moment he stepped forward to allow a server past him, and faced Amanda head on. His mouth dropped open, his dark eyes widened, and he stood rooted to the spot, staring at her with such obvious amazement that her pale cheeks became a delicate pink.

But she collected herself almost at once, gave the man a polite smile and calmly returned his gaze.

He was certainly an arresting physical specimen, several inches taller than six feet with a rangy muscular look and an impressive breadth of chest and shoulders to balance his height. His face was tanned and clean-cut, his dark hair disheveled, his eyes warm and alert as he continued to stare at Amanda. When she smiled, he grinned back automatically, one side of his wide mouth lifting in an engaging lopsided grin that showed a flash of beautiful white teeth.

Amanda always noticed people's hands. This man's hands were hard and brown, probably as callused on the palms as old leather, but they were beautifully shaped, with fine square palms and long fingers.

Amanda looked back to the man's shining dark eyes. She was beginning to feel uneasy. Apparently Mary Gibson was also becoming uncomfortable at the intensity with which the man was staring at Amanda.

"Brock, this is Amanda Walker," Mary said finally. "Amanda, Brock Munroe, my nearest neighbor. He has a ranch right next to mine."

The tall man broke his gaze with a visible effort and extended his hand. Amanda took it almost reluctantly and felt her own hand swallowed in his firm grip. Brock Munroe's hand was just as steel-hard and strong as she'd expected. And she was distressed by the sudden tingle of sexual excitement that shivered through her at his touch.

"Amanda does clothes buying and TV commercials, things like that," Mary explained.

"I know," the man said abruptly. "I've seen her on television."

He was staring again, as if trying to memorize every line and detail of Amanda's face.

Or, Amanda thought in warm confusion, as if they were already well-known to each other, lovers meeting again after a long, long separation...

Mary smiled at them and began to edge away, murmuring something about helping Virginia with the buffet, but Brock and Amanda were so absorbed in their sudden and surprising contact that they hardly noticed her departure.

"So," Brock said with that same abrupt tone, "what exactly is a personal shopping service, Amanda? What is it that you do for a living?"

"I dress people," Amanda said automatically. "I help them to select a balanced complementary wardrobe, and the proper accessories to achieve a total look. And then I price-shop the stores for them, over as wide an area as I'm able, as well as the catalogues from the better houses.''

The man beside her nodded thoughtfully. Amanda looked up at him with a cautious critical eye, noticing for the first time that his suit had to be fifteen years old, at least, with its old-fashioned lapels and the awkward dated cut of the trousers. And that *tie*...

Amanda couldn't help thinking what a shame it was to see a man like Brock Munroe dressed this way. With his beautifully-formed body, he'd look just wonderful in a really well-cut suit.

She stole another glance at his lapels.

"Eighteen years," he told her quietly.

Amanda looked up at his face, startled. "I beg your pardon?"

"This suit. I bought it eighteen years ago for my high school graduation. That's what you're thinking, right? That I look real tacky and out-of-date?"

Amanda flushed and then realized with annoyance that this reaction had been as much of a giveaway as her earlier expression of distaste. "Clothes are my business," she told the man stiffly. "I can't help but notice cut and style. It's my job."

"And you think I've failed to deal with all those tiny intangibles that add up to a total look?"

Amanda glanced up at him sharply again, recognizing her own words in his deep teasing voice. Was she being gently ridiculed by this handsome rustic?

"I wasn't really thinking about your appearance at all," she lied, trying to keep her voice cool. "I'm just enjoying the party, and I was looking for my friends, actually. I think they're out on the patio."

She began to edge away but the man put his big hand on her arm, just below her elbow. To her horror and growing annoyance, Amanda found herself thrilling once again at the warmth and intimacy of that touch.

She jerked her arm and Brock released it instantly. He reached to lift a glass of white wine from a passing tray and handed it to Amanda.

"Thank you," she said, pausing to sip from the crystal goblet, while struggling to compose herself.

"How do you know Mary?"

The question came as a surprise. Amanda hesitated. "Actually, I don't," she said. "We just met today. I have some clothes she's interested in seeing."

The man turned to stare at her. *"Mary?"* he asked in disbelief. "Mary Gibson is hiring a personal shopping service? A professional image-maker?"

Amanda felt another surge of irritation. "Look, Mr. Munroe," she began, "you're certainly free to have any opinion you like about my job. But that doesn't mean that I—"

"What do you like to do?" he asked, ignoring her cool tone. "I mean, when you're away from the job? What kind of person are you, Amanda? You know, I've always thought..." He paused suddenly, looking embarrassed.

"What? What have you always thought?" Amanda asked, intrigued by his sudden discomfort.

"Nothing," the big man said with a casual shrug. "I've always liked to find out what interests people, that's what I was going to say."

"You want to know what *interests* me?"

"Yeah. I want to know what you're like. I mean, do you spend all your time getting your hair done and reading fashion magazines, or do like to jet-set around the world, or what? When you're all alone, what do you dream about?"

Amanda bit her lip and stared at him in silence, thinking about his question.

What did she like to do?

The tall man watched her calmly, apparently prepared to wait all day for her response. But Amanda was slowly realizing, to her growing discomfort, that she had no answer to give him.

She didn't know what she liked to do. The truth was, Amanda Walker hardly knew who she was anymore.

There'd been a time, years ago, when she'd been far more definite about her likes and dislikes. She could remember herself at twenty-one, telling Edward with girlish happiness that she loved running barefoot on the beach, waking early to watch the sunrise across the lake, walking in the woods at twilight and listening to the hushed music of the night birds.

And he'd laughed, gazing at her with raised eyebrows and that wry sardonic grin that had always made her heart turn over.

"My, my," he'd said with the flat New England twang that sounded so sophisticated to her Texas ear. "What an intriguing little savage we have here. The face of an angel and the soul of a hillbilly."

Amanda had flushed with embarrassment at her own naiveté. Instantly she'd resolved to be more the kind of woman Edward admired, more cultured and intelligent and in tune with the nuances and realities of his New York life-style.

And she'd certainly succeeded. During the years that she'd been in New York, Amanda Walker had become the toast of their small exclusive circle, a graceful arbiter of fashion, gifted with a sure knowledge of what was correct for every occasion. She was at ease in any group, comfortable with the casual witty patter that was so much in vogue, secure in the knowledge that she was the most elegant woman in any gathering.

But did she *like* that life?

And if she did, why had she decided to come back to Texas, left Edward behind along with all their friends and embarked alone on this terrifying project?

And it really was terrifying—throwing aside the security of Edward's arms as well as a large salary and expense account, for the dangers and uncertainties of opening her own business.

"I like to succeed," she told the man in front of her with a quick defiant lift of her head. "I like the idea of making my own way in the world, taking on something that's really difficult and making it into a viable and lucrative operation."

She saw something in Brock Munroe's face, a flicker of some emotion that looked almost like disappointment.

"And is that all you dream about, Amanda? Being a big success? Is that your whole happiness in life?"

Amanda met his eyes. Then she flushed and looked away, buffeted by a sudden paralyzing wave of yearning when she remembered her dream.

The dream haunted her all the time these days. She saw herself on a grassy hillside, laughing in the sunlight with a baby in her arms. That was the whole dream, just herself and the midday warmth and the comfortable weight of the drowsy infant in her arms. And somehow there was also the knowledge that a man stood nearby, unseen but deeply loved.

The image was always brief, usually invading her sleep in the misty hours just before dawn, and it filled

Amanda with a happiness so exquisite that waking to cold reality sometimes seemed like an anguish too great to be endured.

She glanced helplessly toward the patio door and saw Beverly emerge, mouthing something and waving across the crowded noisy room.

"I—I have to go," Amanda told the dark man in his poorly fitting suit. "My friends are looking for me."

"In a minute, Amanda," Brock Munroe said gently, holding her with his eyes. "First, you were going to tell me what you dream about."

"I dream about clothes," Amanda told him abruptly, wincing at the harsh arrogant note in her own voice. "And real jewelry and expensive cars. I dream about having lots and lots of money so I can own beautiful things, Mr. Munroe."

When Amanda saw the disappointment that flickered across Brock's face, she was tempted to grab his arm and apologize for her lies. She wanted to say, No, no, it's not true, none of it's true, that's not what I'm like at all....

But maybe it was, she told herself defiantly.

Maybe they were all true, the things she'd just told him. Why was she so driven by her need to succeed in business, if not for the pleasures that came along with financial success? And why had she left behind everything she'd once valued, if not to attain a new goal that meant even more to her?

Brock waited politely, but his handsome face was no longer warm with interest. Amanda wanted to say something—anything to dispel the sudden chill that had come between them.

"Mr. Munroe...Brock, look, I just wanted to..." She began with uncharacteristic awkwardness.

But Beverly reappeared at that moment, waving frantically over the heads of people nearby, trying to catch Amanda's eye.

Conscious of her friend, Amanda paused nervously. Brock smiled down at her with that same distant look of sadness.

"'Again, the Cousin's whistle,'" he quoted softly. "'Go, my Love.'"

Amanda nodded automatically, then turned and stared up him.

"That's from a Robert Browning poem, isn't it?"

Brock Munroe nodded, looking down at her intently. "The poem's called 'Andrea del Sarto,'" he said. "It's always been one of my favorites."

"But..." Amanda's astonishment was evident. "But how..."

"I may be a big simple cowboy in a bad suit, Miss Walker," Brock said quietly. "That doesn't mean I can't enjoy poetry."

She was silent, still searching for words to express her surprise.

"All you glamorous people don't own the world, Amanda," Brock told her quietly, his hard sculpted face empty of emotion. "You don't have a corner on everything that's beautiful and worthwhile. The rest of us may be peasants, but we have eyes and hearts and souls just like you do."

Amanda felt an urgent desire to explain herself, to apologize and show him she wasn't what he considered her to be. But this emotion was soon overridden by a slow burning outrage.

How *dared* he be so superior and judgmental, this "simple cowboy in the bad suit," as he called himself? What gave him the right to express opinions about Amanda Walker, to look at her with such evident disappointment and give the clear impression that she'd been weighed in the balance and found wanting?

"I suppose that's true," she told him coldly. "I really wouldn't know, and I'm not all that interested in finding out, to tell you the truth."

He nodded, accepting her words as a dismissal.

"Goodbye, Amanda," he murmured.

"Goodbye," Amanda said with a small sardonic lift of her beautiful mouth. "It's certainly been interesting talking to you."

Then she was gone, moving gracefully off through the laughing throng, conscious of his dark eyes resting on her as she walked away.

CHAPTER THREE

RAIN POUNDED against the windshield and streamed over the surface of Amanda's small car, whipping past in gusty sprays to pool on the highway and in the ditches. Amanda gripped the wheel, frowning and squinting into the darkness, struggling to see ahead each time the wipers gave her a brief field of vision.

"Damned lousy rain," Beverly Townsend muttered, lounging beside Amanda in the passenger seat and glaring out the window. "It's probably fixing to flood again, like it did in the spring. Everything will be a great big ol' mess, all over again. I hate it, Mandy. I just *hate* it."

Amanda grinned at her friend's fretful tone, distracted for a moment from the strain of driving in the storm.

"Well, I declare, Beverly Townsend," she said in a cheerful imitation of Beverly's warm Texas drawl, "you certainly aren't your usual chipper self tonight, are you? Now, why on earth could that be, I wonder?"

Beverly had the grace to smile back, her teeth flashing white in the darkness. "Well, what do you expect? Here I am, a poor helpless waif thrown out of my own home, forced to thrust myself on the hospitality of a friend who doesn't even like me enough to show the least little bit of sympathy."

Amanda chuckled. She was always charmed by Beverly's witty good humor, and by the warmth and sweetness that were so startling to all those people who looked on Beverly Townsend as little more than a self-absorbed beauty queen.

"Nobody's throwing you out of your home," Amanda pointed out reasonably. "This was entirely your own choice, Bev, coming to Austin to stay with me for a week or so to give Carolyn and Vern some time alone together."

Beverly shrugged. "Well, sure, but really, what choice did I have, Mandy? It's their *honeymoon*, for God's sake. And since Mama absolutely refuses to go away anywhere while Cynthia's so close to her due date, I could hardly hang around the house and make it a cozy threesome, could I, now?"

"What about Lori? Isn't she going to be around? She lives there, too, doesn't she?"

Beverly glanced over at her friend with the look of weary but resigned tolerance that she reserved for Amanda.

"I *told* you," she began, "about twelve hundred times, Mandy, that Lori's been renovating the old garage next to the tennis court to make a gorgeous little studio apartment for herself. It's not quite finished but she moved in a couple days ago anyhow, just to give the newlyweds some privacy.''

''Did you tell me that?'' Amanda asked blankly.

Beverly laughed, then sobered and gazed moodily out at the rain once more.

Amanda stole a sidelong glance at her friend's discontented profile. ''You know what I think? I think this mood of yours has nothing at all to do with the weather or where you're going to be living for the next week, Bev.''

Beverly turned to glance at her quickly, then sank low in the seat and braced her blue-jeaned knees against the dashboard, hugging them gloomily.

''I know,'' she said at last. ''But, Mandy, it's so strange, somehow. All those years I had so much fun playing the field, picking up guys and dropping them just for the hell of it, never really giving any of them much thought. Now, I hate to admit it, but Jeff goes away for a week on business and I can hardly stand it. A week, it seems like eternity, you know what I mean? I don't know if I can bear to be away from the man for a whole entire week.''

Amanda gave her friend a disbelieving look. ''Not even for the chance to spend a week in the city, attend two fashion shows and a gallery opening, meet some really important people and do a whole lot of early Christmas shopping?''

Beverly shook her head morosely. "Nope. Not even for that."

"My goodness," Amanda said seriously, although her mouth was twitching with amusement. "I guess it must be love, all right."

Beverly glared at the other woman and punched her arm lightly. "If you'd ever been really, really in love," she complained, "you wouldn't laugh at my misery. You'd show a little more compassion, you coldhearted witch."

Amanda's face tightened briefly and she stared ahead into the driving rain.

Beverly caught the look and laid a gentle hand on Amanda's suede coat sleeve. "Sorry, kid," she murmured. "I guess you've been through it, too, haven't you? You spent a lot of years with Edward, after all."

"Four," Amanda said, trying to smile. "Four years. And you don't need to treat me like a poor girl with a broken heart, Bev. It was my idea to leave, after all."

"I keep wondering about that, but I never wanted to pry. So there was no big fight or dustup, nothing like that? You just decided to move back to Texas and open your own business, and Edward let you go, just like that?"

"Just like that," Amanda agreed with a sad smile. "All very civilized. He'd just bought his own store in New York, and sunk all the money he inherited into it, and he certainly wasn't about to toss all that aside and follow me, no matter how much he cared about the relationship."

She fell silent, gripping the wheel in gloved hands and gazing bleakly at the black flowing rain.

"And you?" Beverly prodded delicately. "Didn't it hurt to leave him behind after all those years? Did you really want to be on your own enough to give up such a long-term relationship?"

Amanda frowned. "I don't know," she said finally. "I thought I did, Bev. I was getting so restless, so stale and tired of everything, and I really thought I needed a change of scene, some kind of fresh challenge."

Beverly nodded. "Absolutely. That's the way I felt before I got really involved with my hospital work. And Jeff, of course," she added with a faraway smile.

"Of course," Amanda agreed dryly.

"So how do you feel about it all now? Do you wish you were back in New York, working for Edward again and socializing with all your friends?"

"Sometimes . . . well, I guess I do," Amanda said, surprising herself with her response. "Sometimes I feel so lonely and out of place, and so terribly scared that my business will fail and I'll be . . ."

She was silent again, regretting the sudden intimacy of the conversation. Beverly Townsend was a good friend, probably Amanda's closest friend at the moment. But there were things about herself, fears and dreams and longings, that Amanda Walker never admitted to another soul.

Beverly didn't notice the sudden silence. She was still much more interested in the details of her friend's relationship. "So, do you hear from him at all?" she asked.

Amanda shook her head again. "Not often. He said that if we were going to make a break, it might as well be a clean break, but that any time I wanted to come back, he'd be waiting."

"Well, that was real sweet," Beverly ventured cautiously. "Wasn't it?"

"Oh, sure," Amanda said. "Edward always does and says exactly the right thing. Then, about a month later, a mutual friend told me he was dating one of the top models from a big-name agency."

She swerved to avoid the lashing spray of a passing semitrailer, then pulled her little car back into the driving lane.

"It bothered you, right?" Beverly said, glancing at her friend's still face. "Hearing he was with somebody else, it really got to you, didn't it?"

"A little," Amanda said, not willing to discuss the unexpected pain she'd felt when she heard about the glamourous new woman in Edward's life.

"Maybe you're still in love with him," Beverly suggested comfortably. "Maybe you should go back to New York and check it out."

"And give up everything I'm beginning to achieve here? Just admit that it was all a big mistake and go running home saying, 'please look after me, I'm so sorry, I'll never do it again?'"

"Yeah, I see the problem," Beverly said slowly. "Especially since he's not likely to move to where you are, right?"

"Not likely," Amanda agreed bitterly. "He spent years clawing his way up through the retail garment industry in New York to the point where he could manage his own store and draw a handpicked clientele. Believe me, Edward Price is not about to throw all that away for a woman, Bev. *Any* woman."

Beverly was silent a moment, her face thoughtful. "What does he look like?" she asked finally. "You know, I never did meet him, Mandy. Every time I came to New York, he was off on a buying trip to Paris or Bangkok or somewhere."

"I know." Amanda frowned, clutching the wheel and trying to visualize Edward, startled again by the pain it caused her. "He's about five-eleven," she said at last, "thirty-five years old, very handsome and sophisticated. He has hazel eyes and auburn hair that he wears parted on the side and flowing over like this, you know..." She made a quick gesture with her gloved hand against her own dark head, indicating a graceful fall of hair.

Beverly nodded with complete understanding. "*Very* trendy," she said. "Like the guys in the suit ads in magazines, right? I wish I could talk Jeff into getting his hair cut that way. He always looks like his barber lives in the back of a saloon somewhere."

Amanda chuckled, but Beverly's words stirred a chord of memory in the depths of her mind, a thought that had been nagging at her ever since they'd left the wedding party at the Double C and started the forty-mile journey back to Austin.

"Bev," she began slowly, "do you remember that English literature class we took in our sophomore year? I think it was called Late Victorian Poetry, something like that?"

Beverly didn't appear to hear the question. She was gazing out the side window at the neon signs and lighted storefronts that lined the highway for miles on the way into Austin.

"Bev?" Amanda repeated, wondering why this whole question suddenly seemed so important.

"Hmm?" Beverly asked, turning to look over at her friend. "What were you saying, Mandy? Something about college?"

"Our sophomore-year English class," Amanda repeated patiently. "Do you remember it?"

Beverly chuckled. "Who could forget? Old Professor Starcross, with all that awful hair in his ears and the same mustard stain on his tie for the entire term—what a scream."

"Do you remember any of the poetry we studied?"

Beverly opened the glove compartment, rummaging idly for a pack of mints. "I certainly remember the Brownings," she said, popping a mint into her mouth and passing another to her friend. "Robert and Elizabeth, who could ever forget them? Wasn't that just the most romantic thing you ever heard of, Mandy, the way they fell in love just by writing letters to each other and then he went sweeping into her house, gathered her into his arms and carried her away, right under the nose of her awful old father?"

Beverly sighed, lost in the pleasure of the story.

Amanda grinned fondly. "Beverly Townsend, you're an incurable romantic, you know that? As a matter of fact," she added more seriously, "I was interested in one of Browning's poems, not his personal life. I wondered if you might recall it, Bev. It's called 'Andrea del Sarto.'"

Beverly frowned, searching her memory while she munched thoughtfully on the mint. Despite her flippant manner, Beverly had a quick mind and an impressive memory. Amanda was confident she would be able to recall at least something of the poem in question.

"I've got it," Beverly announced finally. "Actually there's two poems, kind of similar, and I always get them mixed up. The other one's called 'My Last Duchess.' But the Del Sarto one, it's about an artist, talking to his wife."

"And it ends with the line, 'Again the Cousin's whistle. Go, my Love.' Right?"

"Right," Beverly agreed. "I always thought that was just about the saddest line in the English language. Tore my heart out, every time I read it."

Amanda felt a brief chill that touched her body with icy fingers, almost making her shiver. "Why?" she asked, keeping her voice light. "You know, I don't really recall the poem at all, except for the title and that one line."

"Well, it's this artist talking to his wife," Beverly began cozily, resting against the door and turning to look at her friend, her blue eyes alight with interest. "She's a whole lot younger than he is, you see, and she's really beautiful and shallow. Completely selfish. He only married her because he was obsessed by her looks, and both of them know it. And in the poem, he's begging her to just sit with him for a while and watch the sunset, but she can't wait to be off with her friends or a boyfriend or whatever."

"Doesn't she love him?"

"Not a bit. She's probably not even capable of love. That's what he's saying in the poem, ever so gently. He's not really complaining about her, just saying how different their lives could have been, what a great painter he could have been and how much happiness they could have had if only she'd had enough depth to care for him a little and give him even the tiniest bit of support."

"But she's just too shallow and superficial,"
Amanda said grimly. "Too interested in herself and
her own looks and nothing else."

"Absolutely," Beverly agreed, missing the sudden edge in her friend's voice. "Mostly, she's just
wishing the boring old guy will quit talking so she
can take off and do what she wants."

Amanda nodded thoughtfully.

"And the last line," Beverly went on, "is because
she's itching to get away from him, you know, and
be off about her own entertainment, leaving him sitting all alone in the sunset. Just to keep the peace,
they're pretending she's going out with her cousin,
but both of them know it's not true. So he talks a
little more about how he feels, all that he's given up
for her and how he feels it's been worth it, just to
have the privilege of looking on her beauty sometimes, even though most of his life is terribly sad and
lonely. And then, finally, he sees that she's anxious
to be gone so he just says that line, ever so gently, the
one about her cousin, and lets her go."

Amanda shivered again. Was that the opinion
Brock had formed of her after just a few minutes'
conversation? Did he really see her as a woman who
was all show and no substance? A woman so shallow and self-absorbed that she would give a man a
life of lonely pain and emptiness?

Her hands tightened on the wheel and she negoti-
ated a corner a little too fast, slamming on the brakes

and sending a sheet of water slashing past the roof of the car. She righted the vehicle just in time to merge unsteadily back into the flow of traffic.

"Wow!" Beverly commented admiringly. "Not bad, Mandy. Since when did you get so reckless?"

Amanda ignored the question, still absorbing the subtle insult of Brock Munroe's final words to her.

"Bev, what do you know about Brock Munroe?" she asked abruptly. "The tall dark-haired man who was Vernon's best man at the wedding?"

Beverly chuckled. "You don't have to describe Brock to me, Mandy. I've known him all my life. In fact," she added cheerfully, "when I was about six and he was sixteen, he rescued me from drowning when we were at a community swimming party down at the river. Actually jumped into a whirlpool, dragged me out coughing and spitting like a drowned rat. Afterward, my parents found out he couldn't swim a stroke himself, he just sort of acted on instinct. I had a terrible crush on him for about five years after that."

"But what's he like, Bev? What kind of family does he have?"

"Poor Brock, he doesn't have a family. Never did, not to speak of. His mama died when he was just young, and his daddy was such a bad apple that Brock did most of the parenting. When he was just a teenager he worked like a man, ran the whole ranch, they say, while his daddy was off drinking and playing cards.''

Amanda thought again of the clear steady dark eyes, the quiet uncompromising look of the man.

''So,'' she began slowly, ''he has no formal education at all?''

''No,'' Beverly said cheerfully. ''A high school diploma, I guess, and that's about it. Poor Brock, he's always just been a hardworking rancher, as long as I can remember.''

''Is he married?''

Beverly shook her head. ''Never has been. Women chase after him all the time, and he sure doesn't mind their company, but Brock Munroe just doesn't seem to be the marryin' kind, if you know what I mean. As far as I can recall, he's never even gotten really serious about anyone.''

''But when he does get serious about someone, what will she be like, do you think?''

Beverly shrugged. ''Who knows? Likely she'll be some nice wholesome ranch girl who can brand a steer and string a fence line, and raise him up a whole brood of curly-haired little kids.''

Amanda was silent, absorbing this image, wondering at her sudden wistfulness and the new thrust of pain that stabbed at her. It was, in fact, quite similar to the pain she experienced when she thought of Edward with his young model. And yet this pain had a different quality about it, something more subtle and hurtful....

"Why?" Beverly asked, rummaging busily in the glove compartment again. "You know, I thought I had some peanuts in here," she complained. "I'm *sure* I...oh, good, here they are. Why all the interest in Brock Munroe?" she added casually, opening the plastic container and pouring a mound of salty nuts onto her palm. "Care for some nuts, Mandy?"

Amanda shook her head in disbelief. "Beverly Townsend, I swear I don't know why you don't weigh two hundred pounds. I'm not interested in Brock Munroe," she added just as casually. "We just got involved in kind of a weird conversation, that's all, and I was really grateful when you rescued me. Guess who else I talked to?" she added brightly, changing her mind and taking several peanuts from Beverly's outstretched hand.

"Who? I thought you didn't talk to anybody. I was sure you just stood alone in that damned corner all night long."

"I talked to Mary Gibson. And guess what, Bev? She wants to look at some clothes!"

"That's great," Beverly said, "but I don't think Mary can afford designer clothes."

"She can't," Amanda said, and launched into her fabrication about the ill client.

For the rest of the trip, missing boyfriends, disturbing poetry, fears and loneliness were all forgotten as the two young women planned the transformation of Mary Gibson.

THEY WERE so beautiful, the ostriches in Mary Gibson's dream. There were always three of them, two females and a big arrogant male, their huge obsidian eyes wise and gentle, their iridescent feathers glittering like rainbows in the hot desert sun. The birds ran and circled Mary, who sat mesmerized by their lofty grace. Then, gradually, the big male began to drift closer and closer to her, his powerful legs churning slowly, his long neck outstretched in invitation.

In the wondering, slow motion of dreams, he finally knelt and allowed Mary to climb on his back, and then they were off, skimming over the desert sands while she clung to his warm feathers, riding the wind and feeling the sun-warmed sand go flashing past in dizzying cartwheels of light. She was so happy in the dream, free of pain and loneliness, free of everything in the world, ears singing, heart pounding with a wild fierce exultation....

Gradually consciousness replaced the dream. Pain flowed in, the old dull ache that was now so much a part of Mary Gibson's life. The ostriches faded, pushed aside by memories of the party at the Double C.

Mary moaned and rolled over in bed, pulling the pillow over her head, trying to shut out the images of her neighbors' pitying faces and tactfully averted glances, of Billie Jo Dumont's smug grin and lush swaying hips. Worst of all was the memory of Mary herself, actually agreeing to look at clothes with that glamorous television lady...

"God help me, I must be crazy," Mary whispered aloud into the muffling depths of the pillow. "What on earth could I have been thinking about? What do I need stylish clothes for?"

She rolled over again, and lay staring at the ceiling, thinking about Amanda Walker's dark classic beauty and her calm sweet air.

Mary admired women who managed to look perfect on all occasions. Mary herself always felt, even when she did dress up, that there was something not quite right, something hanging or bunching or fitted wrong, something smeared or rumpled or clashing with something else.

Of course, she thought, moving restlessly in the wide lonely bed and gazing up at the ceiling, she'd never had much chance to learn how to dress and make herself up. She'd been married at nineteen, and life had been such a struggle in those early years that there was no money for a young ranch wife to think about getting herself rigged up fashionably.

Still, she and Al had been so happy in those days. They spent their time working and building, laughing together in the sunshine, playing with their little girl....

Tears stung in Mary's eyes and burned hotly against her cheeks. She snatched a tissue from the bedside table and dabbed at her face impatiently, disgusted with herself. "I've done enough crying," she muttered aloud, a habit she'd acquired since the dreadful day when they'd taken Al away. "I'm not going to cry anymore, dammit."

But it was hard not to cry when she remembered all the pain and confusion. Thirty-five years of marriage, Mary thought bleakly. All those years of planning and building and loving and caring, washed away in a single moment by a car swallowed up in the dust.

She hadn't been to the jail to visit him, and she didn't know if she ever wanted to, though she'd gotten a couple of letters from him begging her to come, telling her that they needed to discuss urgent business about the ranch.

"Can you imagine Bubba Gibson sitting in prison?" the neighbors were whispering to one another. "*Bubba Gibson,* locked away in some little ol' jail cell, with nothing to look at but four walls?"

And Mary tried sometimes, but she just couldn't. When she pictured her husband he was always outdoors somewhere, striding across the sun-warmed grass in big booted feet or riding out among his cattle herd, casting a fishing line into the river or standing on a hillside in the sunset with the autumn wind riffling his hair.

He deserves every single thing that's happened to him, Mary thought defensively. *He brought it all on himself, and now he's paying, just like he should.*

At least he recognized that, she reflected morosely. He'd refused J.T.'s offer to bail him out, saying he deserved his punishment and he'd take it like a man. Or so J.T. had told her later. But Martin had insisted on ensuring he'd gotten a speedy trial, with the eligibility of parole for good behaviour, especially in light of the fact he'd testified against that horrible man who actually made it his business to murder innocent animals.

As usual Mary found herself making allowances for Al. She'd never been able to stay angry at him. Back in the early years of their marriage, Al used to tease her about it.

"You know your problem, Mary?" he'd say, half joking, half serious. "Your problem is, you just can't stay mad long enough. You wanna tame a wild hard-livin' hombre like me, girl, you gotta be able to stay mad for a week or two, maybe even a whole month, just so I'll learn to behave."

But she never could. All the things he did that hurt and disappointed her would cause brief blowups and then be forgotten, like those summer squalls that passed by without ever really obscuring the sunshine.

Until Billie Jo came along, Mary thought grimly. That had been Al's only major infidelity, at least to her knowledge, and it had been so deeply, painfully humiliating to her, especially when she realized that everybody else knew and pitied her. Sometimes she cried at night, wondering how her husband could do such a thing to her.

"I guess," she murmured sadly to the small stuffed dog on her dresser, "I just got older. I got to be fifty, and that was too old for him. He wanted somebody younger and prettier, that's all."

And he'd certainly gotten what he wanted, Mary thought miserably, remembering Billie Jo Dumont's luscious figure and shining mane of hair, her sexy pouting mouth. How in the world could any fifty-four-year-old woman expect to compete with all that?

And yet, some deeply buried part of Mary stubbornly refused to accept this. She knew that there was more to a woman than hair and hips, and there was a lot more to marriage than exciting sex.

A woman who gave a man thirty-five years of her life was entitled to something in return, and after all this time Mary was finally beginning to feel a slow-growing outrage at the way she'd been treated.

All the neighbors had thought she was being brave and forgiving, Mary thought with a sad smile, levering her small slender body out of bed and dressing rapidly in jeans, shirt and sneakers.

But in actual fact, courage had had very little to do with it. The truth was, she hadn't known what else to do. If she had left her unfaithful husband for good, where could she have gone, what could she have done, with no skills or training of any kind? This ranch had been her whole life, as long as she could remember.

And now, because of Al's terrible foolishness, even the ranch was in danger....

Mary shivered, hugging herself in the cold morning light, her face taut with worry, her hazel eyes bleak.

Finally, drawn by the irresistible smell of bacon and fresh coffee, she hurried into the bathroom and then down the hall to the kitchen.

"Mornin', Mary," Luke Harte drawled, turning from the stove to smile at her, spatula in hand. "Looks like it's fixin' to be a real nice day. Care for an egg this mornin'?"

Mary nodded and poured a mug of coffee for herself from the pot on the counter, grateful for his presence. In the days before Luke came along, mornings had been the worst time of all. She'd grown used to Al being away in the evenings, but she hated getting up alone, planning the day and watching the sun rise without anybody sitting across the table from her.

Luke Harte had drifted in early one morning, just a few days after they took Al away to prison. Mary had answered the door.

"I heard about Bubba," he'd drawled, "an' I figgered maybe you could use a little help around the place, Mary."

"But . . . but I can't afford a salary for you, Luke. There's no—"

"I'm willin' to work for room an' board, an' a little spendin' money on weekends if you can spare it, Mary. Don't worry about it. I'd just welcome a place to live, an' some work to do."

Mary nursed her warm coffee mug at the table, watching him fry the eggs, remembering her startled gratitude and the appreciation she felt for the work he did without complaint.

Luke Harte was a tall, lean young cowboy, probably in his late twenties or early thirties, Mary calculated, with a handsome craggy face and smooth dark hair and moustache. He looked like a young Clark Gable.

People called Luke a drifter, said he'd been in some kind of trouble back in Wyoming, and that he'd already had run-ins with a couple of the local ranchers. Mary knew that he'd lost a job here and there, though she didn't pay much attention to the details.

A few of the neighbors, like Brock Munroe and J. T. McKinney, had even tried tactfully to suggest that maybe Mary should let Luke go, hire somebody else or ask the other ranchers to help out if she needed anything.

But Mary ignored their advice. She liked Luke, who was unfailingly cheerful, and didn't mind doing things like this . . . getting up early in the morning to make breakfast for both of them. He was a good worker, too, and he made Mary laugh.

She enjoyed mothering him, mending his clothes and fussing over his meals. He was, after all, about the age of her own daughter, Sara, who was married and lived in faraway Connecticut.

Hastily Mary smiled her thanks as Luke set a plate of eggs and pan fries in front of her, then sat opposite and reached for the salt.

"If it stays fair, I might run them calves in from the upper forty an' check the ear tags," he commented, "okay, Mary?"

"Okay," Mary said automatically. "We need to do that before I can sell them, and I sure need to sell something. The bank says . . ."

She fell abruptly silent, conscious of Luke's dark eyes resting on her with sudden interest.

"What?" he asked. "What does the bank say?"

"Oh, just the same as always," Mary said lightly, avoiding his eyes as she poured a careful dribble of ketchup over her fries. "Seems the bank always wants money, no matter what. So I guess I'd better sell the calves as soon as I can."

He was silent, his dark eyes still resting on her thoughtfully.

"There's a lady coming to visit, probably on Wednesday," Mary said abruptly, suddenly uncomfortable under his intent gaze.

"Yeah? One of the neighbors?"

"No, actually, it's a lady from the city who's a friend of Beverly Townsend," Mary said carefully, conscious of his sudden tension. "She sells clothes," Mary added, trying to keep her voice light.

"Door to door? Like a vacuum-cleaner salesman?"

"Oh, goodness, no. She's a New York fashion lady, and she helps people pick the right things to wear so they...look good, you know?" Mary concluded lamely, her cheeks flushing with embarrassment.

"Well, that's just pure silly," Luke drawled, his eyes resting on her admiringly. "No fancy New York lady could look any better than *you* do, Mary."

Mary was pleased and flustered by the warmth in his eyes, but at the same time felt a surge of irritation at the blatant flattery. She gave a rueful glance at her faded jeans, her roughened hands with their uncared-for fingernails, and remembered her shapeless graying hair.

"Oh, I expect there's probably a *little* room for improvement," she said dryly. "Anyhow," she added, still flushing with discomfort as she got up abruptly to pour herself more coffee, "she wanted to come out and show me some clothes, and I couldn't see any reason not to look at them."

Luke was silent, his dark handsome face unreadable as he wolfed his breakfast and sipped steadily at a mug of coffee.

"Luke..." Mary began.

"Yeah?"

"Did you ever see an ostrich? In real life, I mean?"

"Sure," Luke said, wiping his mouth and holding out his coffee mug to her for a refill. "A place I worked over in New Mexico, the neighbors raised 'em. Ranched 'em, just like horses. Ugly as sin, them big ol' suckers are. Mean, too. Just as soon kill you as look at you. They can tear a man's guts out with one kick."

Mary remembered her dream, the same one that recurred at least two or three times a week. She recalled the gentle power and dignity of the big male ostrich, the regal grace of the females, the wondrous feeling of being invited to ride those warm feathers to a sun-spangled haven.

"Why?" Luke asked, gazing at her curiously. "Now, what made you think about ostriches, for God's sake, on a nice fall morning?"

"Nothing," Mary said briskly, beginning to clear the table. "Just something I saw on television a while ago, I guess."

She ran a stream of hot water into the sink and sprayed detergent under it, watching the mounds of bubbles rise, conscious of his puzzled dark eyes resting on her rigid back.

Finally he muttered something vaguely polite, placed his cowboy hat on his head and ambled down the back steps and out into the sunshine.

CHAPTER FOUR

BROCK MUNROE TIGHTENED his pliers around a strand of barbed wire, then gripped and tugged powerfully, his big shoulders straining as he worked. When the wire was firm and singing with tension, he wrapped it swiftly around a corner post and braced a staple against the wood, pounding the staple in with two quick strokes to secure the taut strand.

Brock made his way back down the length of fence line, stapling the new wire to each post, sighting along the neat parallel rows to keep the strands level. Then he strolled back through the midday sunlight toward his truck, which was parked near the top of a rugged knoll behind a screen of dusty mesquite.

Alvin trotted at Brock's heels, sides heaving, tongue lolling. Occasionally he fell back onto his plump haunches and delivered a huge gusty sigh, full of weariness and self-pity.

Finally, when Alvin's discomfort grew too noisy to ignore, Brock looked down at the little dog with a cheerful grin.

"Now, just what's going on here, Alvin?" he asked, his brown eyes dancing with merriment. "You trying to tell me something, or what?"

Alvin gazed up at his master with a look of longing, while his tail thumped plaintively on the dusty ground.

"Okay," Brock said, relenting. "Lunch time. C'mon, we don't have to go all the way back home. I brought a picnic."

Alvin's eyes brightened. He brushed past his master, swaying importantly, and raced toward the truck, his ears slanted forward hopefully.

But his face fell when Brock hefted a small paper sack of dog food from the back of the truck and poured some onto a battered tin plate, then took out his own paper-wrapped stack of roast beef sandwiches.

Whistling, Brock strolled over and seated himself on a fallen log, unfolded the sheet of wax paper and began to eat.

Alvin, meanwhile, nosed glumly into the pile of dry dog food and then eyed Brock's sandwiches with a look of bitter reproach.

Brock chuckled. "Feeling cheated, are you, boy?" he asked companionably. "Gawd, Alvin, you're just the most spoiled, greedy little . . ."

But as he spoke he ambled back toward the truck, rummaged behind the seat for a greasy paper sack and extracted a big meaty soup bone, which he tossed onto the grass at the dog's feet.

"There, you monster, let's see you complain about *that*. Nora saved it for you yesterday, down at the Longhorn. Not as if you'd ever deserve anybody being that nice to you."

But Alvin was no longer paying the slightest attention. He fell on the soup bone with passionate excitement, tail wagging frantically, ears flopping in his haste.

Brock watched the dog for a moment, shaking his head ruefully, then returned to his sandwiches.

He smiled, enjoying the warmth of the sun on his shoulders, the crisp tang of autumn in the gentle breeze and the graceful soaring flight of a turkey vulture high above him. The huge bird was just a speck at this distance, circling slowly over the ranch yard off to the east.

Brock leaned forward and peered through the screen of mesquite that crowned the hilltop, gazing down at the same ranch yard. This remote outcrop of land was one that Brock Munroe seldom visited unless he was searching for lost stock or needed to repair the fence. It was also the highest point on his property, and the closest to any neighboring ranch buildings.

In fact, from his vantage point Brock could gaze right down into the Gibson ranch yard, see the house and the comings and goings of its occupants. He watched from behind his bank of dusty greenery, feeling vaguely uneasy as Luke Harte strolled down the back steps and started off in the direction of the corrals, thumbs cocked into his belt loops, rolling cowboy walk clearly discernible even from this distance.

Mary appeared in the doorway and called something to the young man. He paused, turning to reply. Brock could see Luke's teeth flashing white in the sunlight against his sun-browned face and dark mustache, and hear Mary's gentle voice rising on the wind before she vanished back inside the house.

Thoughtfully, Brock settled back against the gnarled tree trunk behind him and munched on an apple, his face troubled.

He didn't like the idea of Luke Harte living down there at the Gibson place with Mary. Even worse, Brock hated the idea that a few local people were already beginning to whisper about the situation, speculating rudely and joking about what might be going on in Bubba's absence.

"Goddammit anyhow," Brock muttered aloud to his dog, who had his nose buried deep in the recesses of the soup bone and was gnawing ecstatically. "People just plumb make you sick, don't they, Alvin? If they have half a chance they'll gossip about anybody, and not even give a thought to how mean they're being."

Brock watched his fat dog devouring the meat on the big bone. He shook his head, still thinking about Mary Gibson.

Mary had always been so kind to Brock Munroe, the closest to a mother that he'd had for most of his life. He could hardly bear the way she'd been suffering, first at Bubba's unfaithfulness, then his disgrace, and now the whispers and slurs from a few of their more uncharitable neighbors.

Of course Mary needed someone to help her run the ranch, Brock mused. She was a proud independent woman, but too gentle and unskilled to do it all alone. And she stubbornly refused to accept offers of ongoing help from the neighboring ranchers, knowing that they were all busy with their own places and her husband might not be coming home for a long, long time.

If ever, Brock thought, remembering the grim look on Mary's face last time she'd mentioned Bubba, or Al, as she always called him, refusing to accept his lifelong nickname. In fact, Mary was the only person Brock knew who called her husband by his given name.

Brock wondered if Mary would let Bubba come home again when he'd served his time, or if she'd just give up on everything, sell the place and go live with her daughter in Connecticut.

Maybe she'd be forced to do that, he thought unhappily, remembering some whispers he'd heard about Bubba's debts, troubles with the bank and several defaulted loans.

"Poor Mary," Brock muttered aloud. "*Damn,* I wish I could..."

But he never finished his thought. At that moment, a small bright red vehicle rounded the stand of live oak trees near the windmill and pulled up in front of Mary's house. Brock took one startled look at the little car and its driver. Then he dived into his truck, rummaging beneath the passenger seat for his hammer and pliers.

At last he found them, snatched them up and moved out into full view on the hilltop, pounding carefully on the stretch of fencing and glancing surreptitiously at the woman in the ranch yard far below, who was now leaning into the back seat of her little car and pulling out many pink-striped boxes and bags.

Brock stretched the wire and pounded staples automatically, gazing with hungry intensity at the view that was being offered him. He saw a pair of long graceful legs in white fitted slacks, delicate curving hips firmly outlined beneath the taut fabric, and a slim waist circled by a narrow gold belt.

Amanda Walker backed out of the car, struggling with another pile of boxes, hopping on one foot and reaching the other behind her with a charming awkward motion to kick the door shut.

She called something to Mary on the veranda and then turned to set her boxes on the hood of the car, laughing in the sunshine, glancing idly up at the hilltop where Brock was silhouetted against his bank of greenery.

When her delicate face turned up toward him, Brock's mouth went dry and his heart began to thunder against his worn denim shirtfront.

This woman, this Amanda Walker was without a doubt the most desirable woman he'd ever met.

And the most shallow and selfish, he told himself grimly, remembering their brief conversation at the wedding.

"I dream about having lots and lots of money so I can own beautiful things..."

Brock waved casually at the women, then gripped a fresh strand of wire in his pliers and pulled on it with great deliberation.

"The one woman in all the world who's born to be my dream come true," he told Alvin in disgust. "The only woman I've ever met who could make me feel that way, Alvin, turn me right inside out. And what kind of person is she? A cold self-centered witch. Now, is that bad luck, or bad management, or what?"

Alvin looked up at his master with miserable dark eyes.

Brock returned the dog's gaze, laughing heartily in spite of himself. Alvin, in his greed, had somehow wedged his entire muzzle deep into the opening of the soup bone and was now trapped, unable to move his jaws. He pawed frantically at the confining circle of bone, struggling to pry it off.

Brock regarded the dog's contortions with scant sympathy. "Serves you right, you little glutton," he muttered. "Maybe we'll just leave that thing right where it is for a week or so and see if you can lose some weight."

Alvin began to run around in tight panicky circles, waving his head and making harsh guttural noises deep in his throat.

Brock grinned and glanced down at the mound of gaily-striped boxes and bags that Amanda Walker was preparing to carry into Mary's house.

"Oh, *great*," he muttered to his unhappy dog, who was still pawing urgently at the trap on his nose. "This is just great. Poor little Mary, in the clutches of a fancy woman like that. As if Mary Gibson can afford to buy a bunch of New York clothes."

The bone popped suddenly free. Alvin heaved a sigh of relief, gave his master a bitter haughty glance and began, more cautiously, to gnaw at the meaty center once more.

Brock turned aside to grin at his dog, then looked down again, watching tensely as Mary descended the steps and approached the smiling dark-haired woman.

Brock was concerned when he saw how ill-at-ease Mary seemed, but being human and a normal healthy male, he couldn't help giving another appreciative glance at Amanda's shapely curving figure in the trim slacks and shirt, the glow on her beautiful face and the way her bouncy dark hair glistened with natural iridescence, as bright as a raven's wing in the warm autumn sunlight.

Dear God, what a woman, he told in himself in awe, pounding staples with a shaky hand. *What an incredible, unbelievable, beautiful woman. If only...*

But his thought was lost suddenly, swallowed up in sympathy for Mary.

She was trying to get out of it, Brock realized, watching his neighbor's fine-drawn weathered face, her shy halting gestures and awkward movements as she spoke to her glamorous visitor, then turned to wave at Brock up by the fence line.

Dammit! Brock thought furiously. Why can't the damned fashion woman just go away and...

But his angry thought was cut off suddenly and he gaped in astonishment as Amanda Walker reached out to enfold the other woman in a warm impulsive hug.

Brock continued to stare in amazement as Amanda held Mary for a long moment, patting her back and murmuring something. Then she turned away with a casual laughing gesture, piled some boxes in

Mary's arms and took another heap herself, walking beside the other woman into the house.

Mary looked much more relaxed after the warmth of that hug. In fact, just before the door closed behind them, Brock was fairly certain that he saw her laugh.

Still shaking his head in wonder, he lowered his hammer and gazed at the lacy blue arch of sky framed among the shifting leaves overhead.

Who was she, this Amanda Walker? What was she really like?

She claimed to want nothing in life but money and luxury, yet she took the time to come and visit a woman like Mary Gibson who couldn't possibly be worth that much of her time. And there was no denying the warmth and spontaneity of that sudden embrace.

Brock frowned, got to his feet and threw his tools into the back of the truck. Finally, without ceremony, he gathered up Alvin, soup bone and all, and tossed him in along with the tools.

Alvin didn't miss a bite, just hit the straw-covered metal deck, skidded into a pile of burlap sacks, then settled back comfortably with the bone still clutched in his jaws. Brock stood and regarded the dog in contemplative silence, fingering his tanned jaw. "Alvin," he said at last, "I think maybe I'd better make a trip into Austin tomorrow. I think I have some business to tend to. Don't you?"

Alvin yawned, revealing the damp black interior of his mouth and an impressive set of shiny white teeth. Then he belched and returned to his careful demolition of the soup bone.

Brock climbed into the cab of the truck, backed around carefully and started down the hill toward his ranch, one denim-clad elbow resting casually on the window ledge.

AMANDA SAT in the comfortable living room of Mary Gibson's home, looking around with interest. The room was warm and casual, just what she'd expected in this big sprawling ranch house. But there were surprising touches here and there—a polished brass bowl filled with autumn flowers and grasses, several delicate watercolors, some exquisite little collector's items that added grace and balance to the decor.

They also revealed something about the woman who lived here, Amanda reflected. Despite her dowdy appearance, Mary Gibson clearly had good taste, and an artist's eye for color and harmony in her surroundings.

Amanda picked up a dainty china horse with windblown mane and tail to examine the beautiful little sculpture, then set it down hastily when the door to Mary's bedroom opened.

Mary moved haltingly toward the archway leading to the living room. She paused, half-hidden behind one of the broad oak pillars.

"Come on," Amanda coaxed gently. "Come right out here and show yourself off, Mary. I'll bet you look just lovely."

Stiffly, her face pale with tension, Mary edged out from behind the pillar and stood in front of the younger woman with her hands folded childishly in front of her.

"Oh, my," Amanda breathed with complete sincerity. "Mary, it's like a miracle. You should see yourself. Did you look in the mirror?"

Mary gave a jerky nod, still appearing on the verge of bolting for cover. But the warmth of Amanda's praise seemed to have relaxed her somewhat. A little color touched her weathered cheeks, and her eyes softened with emotion.

"Turn around," Amanda ordered, getting up off the couch and examining the other woman with a calm professional air. "Let me see the back. I believe the fit is perfect. I don't think it even needs to be touched."

Mary pirouetted stiffly and then looked up at Amanda, her mouth twitching in an awkward smile. "Pretty spiffy, right?" she asked. "Mary Gibson, of all people, in a designer suit."

Amanda leaned over and gave the older woman a small reproving tap on the shoulder. "What do you mean, 'of all people'? Mary Gibson, you have a perfectly elegant figure. A lot of women half your age would envy you that figure. And this suit looks like it was made for you.''

Mary looked down at herself. Her face was still dubious, but her body seemed much more relaxed, and her eyes, Amanda noted, were actually beginning to glow with excitement.

The suit helped, of course. The fabric was a soft cream-colored knit with subtle overtones of heather, almost an exact match with Mary's beautiful light hazel eyes. The skirt draped gently, adding grace and height to Mary's figure, while the brief fitted jacket accentuated her slim waist and shapely hips.

In fact, Amanda realized, Mary Gibson was so close to her own measurements that Amanda's clothes fitted her as if they'd been professionally tailored.

"Made for you," Amanda repeated firmly. "You look all ready for a lunch date at the country club, just as soon as we do something with that hair.''

Mary scrubbed a hand through the lacklustre graying strands. "I haven't been to the hairdresser for months," she confessed shyly. "I've just been hacking it off myself every few weeks.''

"Well, *that's* certainly obvious," Amanda said without sympathy. "Lovely hair like that, and you won't do a thing with it. Absolutely criminal.''

"I should get it tinted and shaped," Mary said. "I know I should. But I always feel so..."

She hesitated, flushing painfully, and smoothed the fine fabric of her skirt with a trembling hand.

"What?" Amanda asked gently. "What do you feel, Mary?"

Mary shrugged and turned away, avoiding the younger woman's eyes. "I don't know," she said at last. "Like everybody's watching and laughing at me, I guess. 'There goes Mary Gibson, poor old fool, trying to make herself look nice while her husband's out running around with a woman young enough to be his daughter....' Amanda, did you *see* that girl's hair?" Mary burst out in sudden despair. "How could I ever compete with that, no matter how many times I go to the hairdresser?"

"Mary, don't say things like that. It's not a competition," Amanda said gently, drawing the other woman down beside her on the couch and putting an arm around her shaking shoulders. "We should never, ever try to compete with other women, not even for our men."

"That's easy to say if you're young and beautiful, and every man in the world wants you."

Amanda gave her a small smile. "I don't think every man in the world wants me, Mary. At least, they're hardly beating my door down at the moment," she added dryly. "But that's not the point. The point is, we should dress for ourselves, not for men. A woman should try to be her best for her own sake and nobody else's, because that's the only way she can feel in charge of her own life. Do you understand what I mean?''

Mary nodded. ''You're saying that I should do this for me, just because it makes me feel good, and not because it might make Al love me again.''

''Exactly,'' Amanda said firmly, turning aside to pick up a sweater so Mary wouldn't see the sudden tears that filled her eyes.

Not because it might make Al love me again . . .

''Now, try the slacks,'' Amanda said. ''The gray ones, I think, with this soft turquoise sweater. I think that color would be really nice on you. You seem to look especially good in subdued secondary colors.''

''Subdued secondary colors,'' Mary echoed with a brave teasing smile. ''Now, I never thought I'd hear words like that in my own house.''

Amanda grinned back, encouraged by Mary's sudden sparkle. A little warmth and interest, a few changes of clothing, and it was already becoming clear what a pretty woman Mary Gibson must have been at one time.

And how attractive she could still be, with some basic attention to detail, Amanda reflected.

''Go,'' she said sternly. ''Go right this minute and put on that sweater and slacks, Mary Gibson, and no more teasing the consultant.''

Mary giggled and vanished obediently toward the bedroom again, her arms full of clothes. But this time she felt comfortable enough to leave the door ajar, calling to Amanda through the opening.

"The gray slacks with the turquoise sweater, did you say? Or this dusty-pink one?"

Amanda paused, thinking. "Either," she called back. "But I think the turquoise will probably be best on you. Or you could try that creamy angora with the fawn-colored slacks."

"Oh good," Mary said with childlike enthusiasm. "I just love that soft cuddly sweater."

Amanda smiled. "Mary," she called suddenly.

"Yes? Oh, Amanda, this angora just feels lovely. It feels like being hugged by something all soft and velvety."

"I know. Mary, that man I met at the party the other night..."

"Which man?"

"The one we were both talking to. I think you said he was your neighbor. His name was Brick, or Brock, something like that," Amanda added with elaborate casualness, as if the man's name weren't burned indelibly into her memory. "Was that him, up on the hill a few minutes ago?"

"Brock? Yes, it was. He's doing some fencing, I guess. What about him? Amanda, should I wear gold earrings or pearls with this creamy color?"

"Gold, absolutely," Amanda said in the direction of the half-closed door. "Pearls will just get lost against that color. I wondered how long you've know him. Brock Munroe, I mean."

"Oh, goodness, all his life," Mary said in a distant muffled voice. "He was just a baby when I came here as a young bride. Brock and I, we sort of grew up together. I always liked that boy."

"He's a strange man," Amanda commented casually, lifting the little horse again and studying it with deep interest. "He even quotes poetry. Seemed completely out of character, somehow."

"Not really." Mary's voice came drifting down the hallway. "Brock's always been a reader. I used to go over there sometimes to visit his mama when he was just a little boy. Brock, he'd always be curled up in a corner somewhere with his nose in a book."

"But he never wanted to get an education?" Amanda asked, setting the little horse down again on a side table. "Why didn't he go to college, if he's so scholarly?"

"He couldn't," Mary said simply. "There was no money in that family to pay for luxuries like college. And besides, he had both his daddy and the ranch to look after. Poor Brock, he's always had to be the..."

Mary's voice grew louder all at once and Amanda looked up to see her standing in the entry. She wore a pair of beautifully fitted camel trousers and the angora sweater, and looked trim and graceful, her face radiant with pleasure.

All thoughts of the enigmatic neighboring rancher vanished from Amanda's mind for the moment. She got up and hurried across the room to hug the other woman, laughing.

"I declare, Mary Gibson, aren't you just pretty as a picture? *Look* what you've been hiding, girl!"

The afternoon drifted away as Mary continued to try on the clothes. They earnestly discussed accessories and shoes, laughing together like schoolgirls.

"Oh, my," Mary said after a couple of hours had passed. "I do believe it's time for coffee. Amanda, this is more fun than I've had in years, and I truly thank you. I don't care what these clothes cost, I intend to buy almost all of them," she added recklessly.

"Oh, they're not going to cost much," Amanda said. "Probably about four hundred dollars for everything you've picked out, and I can always arrange terms if you're—"

"I can afford four hundred dollars," Mary interrupted. "I'm selling most of the calves next week, and I'll just make sure that I get a little of that cash before the bank does."

"But, Mary, if it's a problem . . ." Amanda began cautiously.

"I've worked real hard on this ranch, and I've hardly spent a penny on myself for years," Mary said firmly. "I guess I'm entitled to something that makes me feel this good."

"Of course you are," Amanda said.

Mary looked at the younger woman with sudden shrewdness. "Are you *sure* you're quoting me a fair price, Amanda?" she said. "I haven't shopped for clothes for years and I'm not real sure what things cost nowadays, but this still looks like a lot of good quality stuff for four hundred dollars."

Amanda hesitated, her cheeks growing uncomfortably warm. "You're partly right, Mary," she said carefully. "I mean, you'd never get a deal like this at a retail store. But these clothes are actually secondhand, in a way, since they were bought for somebody else who's decided she doesn't want them. That's why I can give you such a good price."

Amanda settled back, feeling childishly relieved to have gotten through this entire explanation without having to tell an outright lie.

Mary, too, seemed comforted, her face softening into a grateful smile. "Well, it's just wonderful" she said. "For me, it feels like a dream come true. Do you ever dream about things, Amanda?" she asked suddenly, moving toward the kitchen and motioning the younger woman to follow.

"Me? Do I dream?" Amanda echoed, then paused. "Isn't that strange," she added slowly, following Mary into her big sunny kitchen and sinking down on one of the antique oak chairs.

"Strange? What's strange?" Mary frowned briefly, feeling the sides of the coffee percolator, before taking a couple of heavy china mugs from the cupboard.

"Your neighbor...Brock Munroe? He asked me the same thing."

"Brock? What did he ask you?"

"If I dream. He wanted to know what I dream about."

Mary smiled. "What did you tell him?"

"Nothing," Amanda said briefly. "I really didn't think it was any of his business."

Mary nodded, placing the steaming coffee mugs on the table and returning to the counter to fill a plate with oatmeal cookies. "Dreams are private things," she said quietly.

Amanda stirred cream into her coffee, thinking about her recurring dream. The same image had haunted her again in the early hours just this morning. She'd been holding the little baby in her arms and that same man was standing nearby in the sunshine, a man she couldn't see but loved so much that she felt her heart would break with the sweetness of it....

"I keep dreaming about ostriches," Mary said abruptly, her cheeks flushing pink.

Amanda stared blankly across the kitchen table. "Ostriches?"

Mary smiled again. "A pretty strange dream, right? I don't know if I've even seen an ostrich in real life. Maybe once in a zoo, or something. But in my dream, they're so sweet. The big one lets me ride on his back, and we go skimming off across the desert, and it feels so lovely."

Amanda looked at the older woman. "I guess," she began carefully, "that a psychologist would say the birds represent freedom, Mary. Something that can lift you up and carry you away from all your problems."

Mary nodded, gazing into the depths of her coffee mug. "Probably," she said. "Poor Al," she added abruptly. "I wonder what he dreams about, locked away in that jail cell. I wonder if he dreams about being rescued and carried off to freedom."

"Do you still have feelings for him, Mary? Do you love him?"

Mary shifted restlessly in her chair. "I don't know," she said at last, meeting the younger woman's eyes with a frank unhappy gaze. "I truly don't know. I guess you can't spend thirty-five years with somebody and not have some feelings for him, no matter what. I know he did some awful things, and he hurt me real bad, but I still . . ."

She fell silent abruptly, gazing out the window, her eyes carefully averted.

"You still feel sorry for him," Amanda concluded. "You think about him there in jail, with his freedom taken away, and it hurts you."

"Yes," Mary agreed simply. "It hurts me."

"Does he get many visitors there?"

"I don't know. I guess a few of his friends visit sometimes, though it's an awful long way, and I know that Brock's still mad at him for...for what he did."

Amanda was silent, gazing into the depths of her cup.

"And our daughter, Sara, she lives so far away and she's got the kids to look after, but she's hoping to come down at Christmastime and go see her daddy. He'll really like that, seeing Sara."

"How about you? Will you ever go visit him, Mary?"

Mary shrugged. "I guess I'll have to go someday, just to discuss business. The ranch..."

She looked up at Amanda, then down at the table again, picking restlessly at the woven place mat while Amanda waited.

"The ranch isn't in real good shape," Mary said finally. "The bank needs some money right away, and some plans for the future, and I don't have either. I don't know what to do."

Amanda was silent, fighting off the sudden panicky memory of a recent interview with her own banker, of his pursed lips and sober expression while he reviewed her account.

And, although she tried hard not to think about it, Amanda was about to sell Mary Gibson a selection of clothing for four hundred dollars that had cost her, personally, more than two thousand.

But that didn't matter, Amanda told herself firmly. This had nothing to do with business. In fact, the transaction wouldn't even appear in the company books. They were her own clothes, and she could certainly get along without them.

I've got lots of clothes, she thought. *I can spare a few suits and slacks, if it's going to do this much good for somebody else.*

And there was no doubt that the clothes, and the company, had done Mary Gibson a world of good. Her hazel eyes sparkled, her face was animated enough to look really pretty, and she smiled readily despite her obvious concern over finances.

"Nothing cheers up a woman like getting a new look," Amanda said firmly. "It's certainly better than sitting around brooding and worrying. Now if you'll just do something about your hair..."

"Right away," Mary promised. "I'll make an appointment tomorrow. After all, I can't wear those beautiful new clothes with a hairdo like this, can I?"

"Just a light sunny auburn tint," Amanda said, eyeing the other woman with professional interest. "And a soft layered cut, kind of windblown..."

The door opened suddenly. A tall young man entered the kitchen, setting a wire pan of brown eggs on the counter and turning to give Amanda a dark meaningful glance that made her cheeks grow suddenly warm.

"Amanda Walker, this is Luke Harte, who helps out around the ranch," Mary said. "Amanda's brought me a whole lot of the most beautiful clothes, Luke," she went on brightly. "I look like a real fashion plate in them, don't I, Amanda?"

"She certainly does," Amanda said automatically, troubled by something in the young man's stance, by the smoldering depths of his dark eyes.

Mary chattered on, clearly nervous in his presence. "And she's planning to get me fixed up even more. I'm going to the hairdresser, and probably getting my face and nails done besides. Goodness, by the time Amanda's finished with me I'll be able to get a job in *Vogue* magazine."

Luke Harte gave Amanda a cold level glance, his dark eyes unwavering though he addressed his words to Mary. "Well, now," he said in a slow cowboy drawl, "all that stuff's hardly necessary, Mary. You look real good just the way you are. If Miss Walker don't think so, maybe she's not the best person for you to be spendin' your time with."

Amanda gaped at him, speechless with shock and indignation. But before she could form a response he was gone, striding out the door and across the veranda, his boots clattering in the afternoon stillness.

Mary turned to her guest with an awkward smile. "Don't mind Luke," she said. "He's just being loyal and protective of me, that's all. He didn't mean anything by it."

Amanda nodded and murmured something politely noncommittal. After a few minutes she said her farewells. She accepted Mary's check for the clothes, made arrangements to deliver a silk blouse that she'd forgotten to bring, then got into her car and drove away.

Mary Gibson stood on the veranda waving and smiling, her slim figure visible until Amanda rounded the stand of live oak trees and pulled out through the ranch gates and onto the highway.

Amanda waved back before she disappeared, smiling brightly, but she was still troubled by the brief encounter with Mary Gibson's hired man.

Who was he? And was his rudeness really prompted by loyalty and protectiveness toward his employer?

CHAPTER FIVE

BROCK MUNROE STROLLED along the outdoor concourse of the Arboretum, one of Austin's most elegant shopping malls. He smiled in the autumn sunlight, enjoying the pleasant European ambience of the place with its quaint green awnings and flagged walkways.

At last he reached the far end and paused, peering at the sign that adorned a shop window.

SPREE, the sign read, in delicate gold script. "Personal shopping by Amanda."

He hesitated, frowning suddenly. Brock Munroe, despite his rugged cowboy appearance, was a man with a deep love for the written word, and for the nuances of language. Just now he was thinking about the meaning and implication of the word *spree,* the name Amanda Walker had chosen for her business.

A spree was any form of reckless abandonment to pleasure, an orgy of self-indulgence. The word denoted superficiality and wasteful extravagance, both concepts that were completely foreign to Brock's own careful and self-disciplined outlook.

He stared moodily at the elegant little sign, his resolve waning fast. In fact, he was about to turn away and walk back to his truck when he remembered the dark-haired woman's beautiful face and body, and the warm generous spontaneity of the hug she'd given Mary Gibson the previous day.

Finally he drew a deep breath, opened the narrow green-painted door and stepped inside.

Amanda Walker's business office was decorated in hunter-green and cream with touches of dusty-pink and gold. There were a couple of small consultation booths, a long table flanked by high stools and littered with catalogues, a green couch set against a wall covered with fabric samples, and a large desk.

Amanda herself stood at a filing cabinet with her back to him. She straightened and looked over her shoulder, her eyes widening when she recognized her visitor.

"Hello, Amanda," Brock said.

She set a couple of file folders on her desk and came slowly toward him, still silent.

Brock grinned privately when he saw her outfit. She wore baggy gray pin-striped trousers and an oversize black blazer with white shirt and striped tie, a regular man's tie done up in a businesslike knot.

Several irreverent comments sprang to his lips but died instantly when he saw the tension in her lovely face, and the cautious hesitant way she approached him.

And by the time she was near enough to touch, all thoughts of teasing her about the Charlie Chaplin look had vanished from Brock's mind completely. He gazed at her in silent awe, his mouth dry, his head reeling at her beauty.

"Hello, Brock," she said finally, her composure apparently restored. "Are you here to work on your image?"

Brock smiled. "I really doubt that I could afford the amount of work we'd have to do to improve my image, Amanda."

She smiled back, glancing at his clean faded-blue jeans, his white shirt and well-worn brown leather jacket.

"That's highly possible," she agreed soberly.

"Actually, Amanda, I just came in here today to apologize."

"Apologize?"

"It occurs to me that maybe I was a little rude to you the other night at the wedding supper. Maybe I got overly personal when I had no right to, and if you took anything I said the wrong way, I'm truly sorry. I didn't mean to offend you."

She was silent, gazing up at him with thoughtful blue eyes, obviously weighing his words. "I looked up that poem," she said at last, her cheeks tinted suddenly with pink as delicate as mother-of-pearl.

"Poem?"

"'Andrea del Sarto,'" Amanda said. "The line from the Browning poem you quoted to me. I looked it up as soon as I got home."

"And?"

"And you certainly weren't being very flattering," she said, her blue eyes dark with emotion as she looked at him. "In fact, you made a pretty rapid and uncharitable assessment of my general character, didn't you?"

"You're right, Amanda," he agreed calmly. "I think I probably did. That's why I came to apologize. Let's just forget that whole encounter and try again, okay? Let's see if we can do it better next time."

"Next time?"

"Yeah," Brock said, gazing down at her intently. "Let me take you out to dinner some evening, and I promise I won't be rude anymore."

She hesitated, standing there in her ridiculous outfit that somehow managed to be enormously flattering. The baggy clothing gave her a winsome, fragile appeal that Brock could hardly resist. He wanted to gather her up in his arms, carry her over to the green-striped couch right there beneath the fabric samples and make love to her for about ten hours.

"I really don't think that would be wise," she said finally.

Brock stared at her, still caught up in his daydream.

"It wouldn't?" he asked blankly. "Why not?"

"Because we have nothing in common, Brock. Nothing at all. And I think that trying to spend an evening together would be an uncomfortable experience for both of us."

Brock gathered his unruly thoughts. "Well, I think you're wrong," he said calmly. "I think we have a lot in common."

Amanda gave him another quick startled glance. "Really? Like what?"

He held up a brown callused hand, ticking items off on his fingers. "Number one, we know a lot of the same people. Two, we're both in business for ourselves, trying to make a go of it in a tough economy. And three, we read the same poetry."

She smiled suddenly, a sweet shining smile that transformed her face and rendered him speechless once more.

Brock gazed at her, dry-mouthed and shaky with longing, his heart hammering noisily against his shirtfront.

"All right," she said, still smiling. "You've convinced me, Brock. Is tonight okay for you? Let's go out to dinner just to show there's no hard feelings."

"Great," he said, trying to keep his voice casual. "You name the time and place."

"All right," Amanda said again, giving him a be-mused glance, as if she couldn't believe she was ac-tually doing this. "Is eight o'clock all right? I have an appointment here at seven, and you could pick me up afterward."

Brock calculated rapidly. It was midafternoon now. To pick her up at eight, he'd have to drive home more than forty miles, rush through all the evening chores and feed Alvin, then change his clothes and drive forty miles back. And he'd have to remember to...

"Brock?"

"Sure," he said hastily. "Sure, that's fine. Eight o'clock is great. I'll see you then."

He took her proffered hand and held it for a mo-ment longer than was absolutely necessary, drown-ing helplessly in the blue depths of her eyes. Finally he managed to extricate himself and hurried out, striding through the door and down the walkway, still feeling those beautiful eyes resting on him with a warmth more sweet and compelling than the sunny Texas sky.

AMANDA SKIMMED along the freeway in the waning afternoon light, glancing nervously at her watch. She frowned and switched lanes with automatic skill as she juggled appointments in her head. There was just time to slip by her apartment, change her clothes and touch up her makeup before the last two appointments, but she was cutting it pretty fine.

Still, she wanted to wear something different for the evening ahead.

She frowned again, craning her neck to glance in the rearview mirror. Then she settled back into the driver's seat and drummed her fingers restlessly on the wheel.

She felt a growing uneasiness about the prospect of a date with Brock Munroe, and a bitter anger with herself for getting involved in something so ridiculous.

What on earth were they going to talk about for three hours? Despite his skillful protestations, what did they really have in common, the two of them? The man was just a crude outdoor type with callused hands and rough speech, a rancher who lived his life by the sun and seasons, and who knew nothing of the social niceties that governed Amanda's existence.

But, forcing herself to be honest, Amanda was able to admit to herself that his rugged exterior and lack of education weren't what really bothered her the most about Brock Munroe.

If the man would just acknowledge his own shortcomings and be properly respectful, show that he looked on Amanda with a kind of reverent and awed worship for her grace and sophistication, she could probably forgive him his rough edges. The most irritating thing about Brock Munroe was the fact that, though he made it clear that he found Amanda physically attractive, he seemed to look at her with a kind of mocking judgment. His shrewd humorous appraisal always left her feeling defensive and angry.

These clothes, for instance. Amanda had actually felt quite jaunty and stylish when she dressed this morning. But when Brock Munroe looked at her outfit and she saw the merriment that sparkled in his dark eyes, she felt gauche and ridiculous, like a schoolgirl trying hard to be chic.

Still confronting her feelings with the honesty that was part of her makeup, Amanda found that she was disappointed in herself for her reaction to Brock Munroe.

If she didn't have the confidence to defend herself and her life-style against this man's mockery, then why was she living this way? And if she *did* believe in herself, then wasn't it cowardly to avoid the man just because he made her question her choices? Amanda Walker had no stomach for cowards.

So she'd accepted his invitation. And now what was she doing? Running home to change her outfit because she'd caught him looking amused at the clothes she wore.

Amanda shook her head as she turned off the highway. She drove along the city streets to her apartment, pulled into her parking spot and hurried across the lobby to the bank of elevators.

Just one evening, she thought. She'd give him this one evening, dazzle him with her charm and graceful sophistication, and leave the poor man flattened and painfully aware that a woman like Amanda Walker was completely out of his league.

Then she'd never have to see him again.

But even as she framed this thought, she had a vivid memory of the man's muscular body filling her little office, his handsome face and appealing disheveled hair, his brilliant dark eyes. She saw his finely molded brown hands, and shivered at the thought of those hands touching her, stroking her hair and caressing her face. . . .

"Oh, God," Amanda muttered aloud, gazing with unseeing eyes at the brass panel of elevator buttons. "What a fool I am. What an absolute certifiable idiot."

One of her neighbors, a tall military-looking gentleman with silver hair and mustache, glanced up in surprise when he heard her voice, then moved beside her into the elevator when the door opened. He stood calmly in the corner, holding a large potted plant while Amanda punched the button for their floor.

"Talking to yourself, Amanda?" he inquired politely. "Not a good sign, I'm afraid."

Amanda smiled. "Sorry, Mr. Smithers. I've been a little preoccupied these days. There's a lot of pressure out there, you know."

Robert Smithers shook his head sadly. "What a shame. Look at you. Young and lovely, a dear sweet girl with a good education and the world at your feet, and what do you do? You burden yourself with pressure. You should be dancing till dawn every night, drinking champagne from your slippers and having a wonderful life."

Amanda gave her elderly neighbor a fond smile. "I'm afraid those days are gone forever, Mr. Smithers. But it does sound lovely."

They got off the elevator together and parted at Amanda's door. She watched him proceed down the hall, shoulders erect, then she let herself into her foyer and shrugged off her topcoat.

The message light was blinking frantically on her machine. Amanda pressed the button and moved into the bedroom, stripping clothes off as she went, leaving the door open so she could hear the messages.

The bank manager wanted to see her again, but it didn't sound ominous, just some papers she'd forgotten to sign when she refinanced her business loan. A parcel was waiting for her at the post office, and another at the bus depot. Her mother wanted her to call Dallas, and Beverly reminded her that she, Beverly, was going to Houston for a few days with Connie, a mutual friend, to do some Christmas shopping and possibly meet Jeff on the weekend.

"Christmas shopping!" Amanda scoffed aloud, spraying her neck and breasts with cologne. "If Jeff's in Houston, I really doubt that Christmas shopping is Beverly's main concern. I think..."

"Hi, Angel," a familiar voice said, shocking her into silence.

Amanda stood still for a moment, one hand covering her mouth, blue eyes wide. Then she dropped her blouse on the floor and came slowly out into the hallway, staring at the machine.

"It's Thursday afternoon, about two o'clock," Edward went on, his flat New England vowels very pronounced, as they always were in a recording.

"Edward," Amanda whispered.

"I'm in New York, at my office, and I assume you're out getting rich and famous," he went on. "Just wanted to let you know that I'll be in Austin tomorrow. My plane lands at four o'clock and I expect you to be at the airport showing some enthusiasm for my arrival."

"Four o'clock," Amanda repeated, feeling dazed, trying frantically to think through her Friday schedule of appointments.

"I also wanted to warn you," Edward went on calmly, "that I don't intend to leave Austin without you, Angel. You've proved your point, and I give you full marks for your intelligence and enterprise.

But I need you here to take over as my head buyer. And I need you for other reasons, too," he added, his voice dropping intimately, taking on a sudden husky inflection that made Amanda shiver.

Oh, God, she thought. Edward...

"So I'll look forward to seeing you, darling," he concluded briskly, all the disturbing tenderness vanishing from his voice. "We've got a lot to talk about."

The machine beeped and whirred, and went silent. Amanda stared at the instrument as it rewound, her mind whirling rapidly.

Edward was coming to Austin. Tomorrow at this time he'd be here, back in her life, probably right here in her apartment.

Feeling dazed, Amanda stood in the hallway and looked around her.

At least, she thought with a brief smile, Edward was going to like her apartment. He'd definitely approve of this cool decor, the urban minimalist look that Amanda had first learned from him.

"Forget *cozy,* Angel," Edward had told her long ago. "We don't strive for a cozy look. We strive for a cool look. We don't want our visitors to feel comfy and at home. We want them to feel a little chilled, and ever so slightly intimidated by our good taste."

"Why?" Amanda had asked, back in those bouncy innocent days when she still occasionally questioned Edward's pronouncements.

"Because," he said, giving her one of his wintry smiles, "that's how we retain the upper hand, my darling. And retaining the upper hand is vital in all relationships. You'll learn that, you sweet child, as you get older and more cynical."

Edward had certainly retained the upper hand in their relationship. In fact, it wasn't until Amanda had torn herself away from him and begun struggling to make a life of her own that she realized how much influence he'd had over her. The way she dressed, the shows she went to, the furniture she chose, even the friends she associated with, were all selected on the basis of what Edward might think.

And even now, though he was far away in New York, it seemed that his dry wit and impeccable taste still governed most of her decisions.

Amanda wandered through the living room with its pearl-gray carpet and sparse furnishings of charcoal leather and gleaming stainless steel.

"Not cozy, Edward," she murmured aloud, fingering the black metal stem of a tall floor lamp with a big naked bulb. "Definitely not cozy."

She switched on the lamp and stood gazing at it, picturing Edward, recalling his fine patrician features, his compact graceful body and elegantly barbered hair.

There'd been a time when just the thought of that handsome aquiline profile could send shivers all through her body, make her feel weak and shaky with desire. Edward Price had always seemed so much older and wiser, so glamorously suave and sophisticated, so much the essence of everything Amanda longed to be.

When he first noticed her, began asking her out, took her to bed and finally invited her to move in with him, Amanda had been utterly swept off her feet. Years later, she'd still remained almost completely captive in the man's spell, his graceful charm and smiling hard-edged power.

But gradually she'd begun to resist that power, to fight the sense of being swallowed up and destroyed by Edward. Finally, in her mid-twenties, Amanda began to fight him as well, making a tentative effort to assert herself and develop her own personality, to create a tiny private world for herself that was separate from Edward's influence.

The ultimate result of that struggle had been the move to Austin. But if she'd hoped for resistance and pleading from Edward Price, Amanda had certainly been disappointed. He had let her go without a fight, because Edward didn't believe in fighting.

"Conflict is so destructive," he always said. "It puts ugly lines on your face, Angel. Never fight if you can walk away."

That was Edward's style. He always just walked away. Graceful and unsullied by messy arguments, he moved serenely forth to conquer new fields.

Yet now, incredibly, it seemed that he wanted her back. Amanda crossed the room, still in her lacy bra and panties. She curled up in the cold depths of a gray leather chair and shivered at the touch of the bare metal arms against her flesh.

She'd never expected Edward Price to invite her back into his life. In fact, he'd told her as much.

"I don't beg, Angel, and I don't follow. If you want to come back, let me know. Otherwise, have a nice life, my sweet girl."

And now he was coming to see her. He'd even broken down sufficiently to admit that he *needed* her, both in his business and in his bed.

Amanda shivered again, wishing there were a soft cushion somewhere in the room that she could hug for comfort. But the whole apartment was spare and elegant, devoid of any superfluous touches like cushions and knitted afghans that could detract from the classic beauty of chrome and leather.

"Cozy might be nice, actually," she muttered aloud, her blue eyes rebellious. "In fact, I could definitely stand a little touch of cozy, right at this minute."

Suddenly she remembered her dinner date. Edward's message had driven Brock Munroe completely from her mind, but now he was back, his tanned face hovering at the edge of her consciousness, regarding her with a teasing sardonic grin.

Amanda flushed with irritation and got up quickly, wondering if she could phone him and cancel their evening. Probably not, she decided. Even if she caught him at home, he'd likely be outside somewhere on his ranch, doing whatever cowboys did in the late afternoon.

Besides, when she thought about cancelling the dinner date she felt a puzzling stab of disappointment that surprised her. Surely she wasn't looking *forward* to having dinner with that man? Especially when the love of her life was due to arrive within twenty-four hours?

I just need something to get me through the evening, Amanda told herself firmly. *Something to fill in the time till Edward gets here. And it might as well be Brock Munroe, since Bev's out of town....*

She got up and walked quickly back through the apartment, heading for her bedroom. As she went, Amanda looked around and felt her rebellion slowly ebbing away.

She was glad she'd decorated her apartment like this. Edward was going to be seeing it tomorrow, and he would be so impressed.

CHAPTER SIX

"THIS IS SUCH a marvelous steak," Amanda said after swallowing a vigorous mouthful. "It just melts in my mouth. Is yours good?"

Brock nodded and smiled across the table at her. He liked women who enjoyed their food, who didn't pick and poke and nibble. And in spite of her dainty appearance, Amanda Walker had tucked into her steak and baked potato with the enthusiasm of a ranch hand.

Amanda caught his glance and smiled back, her eyes shining like blue stars in the muted glow of the candle between them. "I know I'm eating like a pig," she said cheerfully. "But I didn't have time for lunch, and I'm just starved."

"I love it," Brock said sincerely. "I love watching you eat. Nobody but Alvin enjoys food that much."

"Alvin?" she asked, sipping from her crystal wineglass.

"My dog," Brock said. "He's one of a kind. In fact, I can't describe him, so you'll just have to pay me a visit sometime and meet him for yourself."

She fell silent, looking down at her plate while Brock continued to gaze at her.

Amanda seemed different tonight, awkward and a little constrained, as if she had something on her mind. Her manner toward Brock was subtly altered, too. Throughout the evening she appeared to alternate between holding him at arm's length and wanting to confide in him. She seemed alarmed and uneasy whenever he hinted at the possibility of further contact between them.

Brock felt an upsurge of tenderness, realizing that despite her glamorous appearance and calm poised manner, Amanda Walker was probably a rather lonely person. She never mentioned any close relationships, other than her old college friendship with Beverly Townsend. And she sounded a little wistful when she talked about Beverly and her boyfriend, Jeff Harris.

He studied her bent head with its glossy cap of clipped dark hair, her lovely complexion and the fine delicate structure of her face and neck.

She wore an outfit completely different from the jaunty suit he'd seen earlier. Tonight her dress was a soft blue wool, exactly the color of her eyes and exquisitely tailored with clean flowing lines, a wide grey leather belt at the slim waistline and a prim high neck that made her look more enticing than ever.

"Do you have family, Amanda?" Brock asked abruptly. "Anybody around here who's close to you?"

She shook her head. "My parents live in Dallas," she said. "My younger sister, too. And I have an older brother out in California who's a stockbroker."

"Middle-child syndrome," Brock said with a teasing grin. "No wonder you have such a drive to succeed."

She looked at him in surprise, then grinned back. "You could be right," she said.

"Were your parents really rich?"

"Oh, goodness, no," Amanda said, digging into her baked potato again. "They're both teachers," she added, "but my mother didn't work after we were born."

"An old-fashioned girl," Brock observed.

Amanda shook her head and paused to swallow, then took a sip of water. "Not really. My mother would have loved to work, because she always wanted a really nice home and a kind of elegant lifestyle. But my brother and I were born fairly close together, and then my sister came along and she was born with spina bifida...do you know what that is?"

Brock nodded. "I know all kinds of stuff, Amanda," he told her gravely. "I read all the time."

She nodded again, her cheeks flushing a little. "Well, my sister needed constant care when she was little, so Mom couldn't go back to work. She always tried so hard," Amanda said with a small wistful smile, her blue eyes faraway. "She played classical music on the stereo at mealtimes and set the table with real linen, tried so hard to maintain a certain standard even without money. But it was such a struggle."

Brock looked thoughtfully at the lovely face across from him, wondering at the forces and influences that had shaped this woman.

"How is she now?" he asked finally. "Your sister, I mean."

"Oh, Sarah's fine. She's done far, far better than anybody ever expected. She's still in a wheelchair, but she lives in a little apartment with a friend, and she's almost fully independent. She's going to college in Dallas."

"Good for her," Brock said warmly. "I love to hear things like that."

Amanda smiled back at him. Their eyes met and held for a long moment before Amanda's smile faded and she looked down, then picked up her fork again, her hand trembling slightly.

Brock watched her in thoughtful silence. "How about your mother?" he asked. "Did she finally go back to work and buy all the nice things she craved?"

Amanda shook her head. "I really thought she would, once she was free of her responsibilities. But you know, while Sarah was growing up my mother got involved in a lot of activities for disabled children and their families. And now, when she'd finally be able to do anything she wanted, she's busy with volunteer work just about full-time."

"So she never got the crystal chandeliers," Brock commented.

Amanda glanced at him with that same wide-eyed startled expression she seemed to have whenever he showed any kind of insight or sensitivity.

"No," she said slowly. "Mama never did get all those luxuries she craved. But it doesn't seem to matter anymore."

"Except to you, maybe," Brock said. "You're the one who still wants the crystal chandeliers, aren't you, Amanda?"

She toyed with the sprig of parsley at the edge of her plate, her face thoughtful and still. "I guess I do," she said finally. "It always hurt me so much, seeing my mother sacrifice and do without, knowing how she longed for the nice things she couldn't afford. All the time I was growing up, I told myself I'd never be like that. I wasn't going to spend my life yearning for things and not having them."

"So you went to New York."

"As soon as I graduated," Amanda said. "I was going to make a big splash in the fashion industry, and get rich and famous. But you know what? It wasn't that easy," she added, giving him a cheerful self-deprecating grin that made him want to gather her in his arms and kiss that sweet curving mouth.

"Why not?" Brock asked, forcing himself to sound casual.

Amanda shrugged. "Well, I was too small for modeling, and not creative enough for design. All I had was a kind of instinct for the right look, so I moved up through all the different levels of retail sales and finally got to be assistant buyer."

"Why did you leave, after getting that far?"

She shrugged and looked down at her plate again. Brock watched her curiously, surprised by her reaction.

"Amanda?" he prodded gently.

"Well," she began with some reluctance, "I got into a relationship with a co-worker, and after a few years it wasn't really... going anywhere, you know? I wasn't even sure it was good for me. I felt stale and discouraged, and I wanted some kind of personal challenge. So I finally decided to come back to Texas and go into business for myself."

"How the hell could he let you go?" Brock asked abruptly.

"I beg your pardon?"

"This co-worker. The guy you had the relationship with. You were together for years and then he just let you walk away without putting up a fight?"

Amanda nodded. "He doesn't believe in fighting. He always said that if I wanted to leave, that was my business, and if I ever wanted to come back, he'd be glad to see me.''

Brock gazed at her in stunned amazement, then shook his head slowly. ''I can't believe it,'' he said at last. ''I can't believe any man who had someone like you would just let her go. If that was me, I'd move heaven and earth to hang on to her.''

Amanda gave him a wistful gratified look, then shook her head. ''Maybe I'm not all that terrific when you get to know me,'' she said. ''Besides, it wasn't a great relationship for either of us at the time. He's ten years older than me, for one thing. I felt stifled by him, and I think he was a little bored by me.''

''Bored?'' Brock asked in disbelief. ''By *you?*''

Amanda gave him another of those little sad smiles. ''Look,'' she said abruptly, ''I'm not nearly as fascinating as you seem to think I am. To Edward, I was just a clumsy country girl who had to be taught the proper ways to speak and behave. I think that part was kind of a challenge for him, but once he had me all polished, I wasn't really interesting anymore.''

''A classic Pygmalion,'' Brock commented, then grinned at her reaction. ''Amanda,'' he said gently, ''could you please try not to look so amazed whenever I say anything a tiny bit intelligent? It's not all that flattering, you know.''

Amanda flushed painfully. "Sorry," she whispered, trying to smile. "I know how rude it is of me. It's just that I never expected..."

"I know," Brock said, waving his hand casually. "No need to be embarrassed. I'm just a rough ol' cowboy who doesn't even own a decent suit, and it's understandable that you'd have some stereotyped idea of what I'm like. But," he added gently, "like I told you before, even cowboys can read and think, Amanda. In fact, there's lots of time to read during those cold rainy winter evenings on the ranch."

She was silent throughout this little speech, sipping her wine thoughtfully and giving the waiter a polite smile when he set a plate of chocolate layer cake in front of her.

"Wow," Brock said with warm admiration, watching her pick up her fork. "Dessert, too. What a woman."

Amanda giggled. "You're so different from Edward," she said. "He hated watching me eat. He always complained that it was embarrassing to dine out with a lumberjack."

"You're kidding."

Amanda shook her head, then took a bite of the cake. "Oh, Brock, this is *wonderful!* You wouldn't believe how delicious it tastes. Come on, order a slice for yourself."

The waiter reappeared as soon as she spoke, casting Brock a questioning glance while he removed a basket containing an uneaten slice of garlic toast.

Brock grinned and shook his head. "Sorry. Maybe just some lime sherbet, please. Amanda, you're a genuine marvel."

He watched her enjoyment of the rich dessert, delighting in her beauty but irritated by what she'd told him about her lover.

"Dining out with a *lumberjack*," he muttered at last, unable to contain himself. "What a thing to say to a woman like you."

Amanda set down her fork and looked thoughtfully at the man across the table. She hesitated, sipped her coffee, then apparently made up her mind to confide in him.

"He's coming," she said abruptly.

"Beg your pardon?"

"Edward. He's coming here tomorrow to see me. He left a message on my machine this afternoon."

Brock felt a brief chill, and then a spreading heaviness that he was afraid to analyze. "No kidding," he said lightly. "Are you excited about that?"

"I don't know," Amanda murmured, her head bent so he couldn't see her eyes. "I mean," she added, glancing up briefly, "of course it'll be nice to see him again after all this time, and hear all the news from the city. I'm just not sure if I want to..."

"What?" Brock prompted when she hesitated. "You're not sure if you want to do what?"

"Start all over again," Amanda said quietly, her fingers tracing the outline of her cup handle. "I don't even know if we can."

Of course you can't, Brock wanted to shout. *Especially with a guy who calls you a lumberjack because you have a healthy appetite. You left him once, don't let him back into your life. Keep yourself free, girl.*

But he knew it would be unwise to voice these opinions. Instead he eased the conversation into safer territory, entertaining her with a long funny story about Alvin's morbid fear of cats.

Amanda laughed aloud, her lovely face so animated that once again Brock had to fight a strong impulse to reach across the linen-covered table and gather her into his arms.

"I'd love to meet Alvin," she said. "He certainly does sound like a true original."

"Oh, Lord, I hope so," Brock said fervently. "I'd hate to think there might be another Alvin running around out there somewhere."

Amanda chuckled again and paused to sip her coffee. "How big is your ranch?" she asked after a moment's silence. "Is it like the Double C?"

Brock grinned. "Not yet. I've got some work to do before I get to that stage."

"What do you mean?"

"Well, for one thing, I've only got about half as much land."

"How much is that? I mean, Beverly's told me how many acres they have at the Circle T but I can never really visualize how much land an acre is."

"Well," Brock told her, "six hundred and forty acres make one square mile. So with five and a half thousand, my ranch totals close to nine square miles. The Double C has almost twice that much land."

Amanda stared at him, wide-eyed. "Come on, Brock. You're just teasing me because you know I'm a city slicker."

Brock shook his head. "Not a bit. Actually, at nine sections my place is just medium by Crystal Creek standards. But it's still a nice working ranch. At least," he added with a wry grin, "it will be once I do a hell of a lot more work."

"Your father..." Amanda began hesitantly and then paused, her cheeks once again showing that faint flush that always betrayed her discomfort. Brock looked at her intently, wondering how much she'd already been told about him.

"My daddy was no ball of fire," he said gently. "It's taken me years to get the place into a good working position, and it'll take more years to get it showing a real strong profit. It'll take some diversifying, too," he added grimly, "and a lot of penny-pinching. But I'll get there."

"What will you do first?"

Brock grinned. "First? Good question. Well, I wish I could get done renovating my house, but I seem to be kind of stuck."

"Renovating?" Amanda said, her eyes brightening. "Are you doing that right now? I love the idea of renovating," she added with an awkward little smile. "Sometimes I really wish I'd gone into interior design instead of clothing."

"Lord, girl, if you want a real challenge, why don't you drop out and pay me a visit someday? That's what I need, actually, some advice on design and things before I can go any further."

"Really?" she said, tentatively.

"Hey, I mean it, Amanda," he urged. "Sometime when you're out our way, why don't you stop by for a cup of coffee and tell me what to do with my kitchen? I'd surely appreciate the help. Hell, I'd even pay."

Amanda smiled. "I'd love to," she said with evident sincerity. "And I certainly wouldn't charge you. I'd just do it for fun."

"Now, that's sure the wrong way to do business."

"I know," she said. "But I'm not even sure what's the right way, Brock. These days, it's so hard to do business at all."

He nodded in silent agreement, spooning up mouthfuls of the lime sherbet.

"You know who I feel sorry for?" Amanda said suddenly.

"Who?"

"Mary Gibson. If it's tough for a young strong man like you to make a living on a ranch, how is poor Mary ever going to manage? I guess she has a lot of debts to start off with, and apparently she doesn't know all that much about running the ranch even though she's lived there most of her life."

"That's true," Brock said. "Bubba, her husband, he was always a real take-charge kind of guy. He believed the little woman should be in the kitchen with her apron on, cooking up a good supper for her working man. I doubt that Mary was ever very much involved in decision making."

"And now she has to do it all herself, and she's alone there."

"Not entirely," Brock said, remembering young Luke Harte's shambling figure down in the Gibson ranch yard.

Amanda gazed across the flickering candle. "You're talking about that hired hand of hers? Luke something, isn't that his name?"

Brock nodded. "Luke Harte. You met him?"

"Just briefly." Amanda paused. "It wasn't all that pleasant. He was quite rude to me," she confessed, meeting Brock's eyes. "Mary apologized for him and said he was just being protective of her."

Brock hesitated. "Well maybe he was," he said at last. "I know he's been a lot of help to Mary since Bubba left. I just..."

"What?"

"I don't know," Brock said at last. "I don't like the whole idea, that's all." He looked up, meeting Amanda's gaze again. "People are gossiping about them," he said abruptly.

Amanda stared. "About *Mary?* And Luke Harte? You're joking, Brock. Why, he can't be much older than I am. He's certainly twenty-five years younger than Mary, at least."

"That doesn't stop people from talking. There's a certain kind of people, Amanda, who'll talk about anybody, any mean ridiculous story they can think of, just to be gossiping. God, I hate it."

"So do I," she said. "Especially when it's aimed at somebody like Mary, who's just so sweet."

"She's always been real good to me," Brock said. "In fact, she was like a mother to me when I was a boy. I used to talk to her a lot when I was growing up."

He hesitated, watching as Amanda pursued the last crumbs of her chocolate cake. Then he asked abruptly, "Did you sell her some clothes? Mary, I mean? Did she buy anything from you?"

Amanda nodded. "Quite a lot. Two nice designer suits, and some really good slacks and sweaters. Oh, and a couple of silk blouses, one that I haven't delivered yet."

Brock looked at her in surprise. "I wouldn't have thought Mary could afford that kind of thing," he ventured cautiously.

"Why not? Those clothes cost her less than four hundred dollars altogether. That's not a lot of money for good designer fashions."

Brock's dark eyes reflected his disbelief. "Come on, Amanda," he said slowly. "What gives?"

She glanced up at him, startled and defensive. "I don't know what you mean."

"I was looking in shop windows at ladies' clothes when I walked down here," Brock said. "I saw what they cost. How could Mary buy all those things for that little money?"

"I was . . . actually, I was able to give her quite a good deal," Amanda told him stiffly.

"Yeah," Brock drawled, looking with thoughtful interest at the woman across the table. "Obviously you were."

But from the shuttered expression on her face, he guessed it would be dangerous to pursue the matter. Instead he scooped up the check, helped his companion into her silk jacket and followed her from the restaurant, conscious that every man in the room was watching Amanda Walker with admiration as she moved quietly among them, her dark head high, her dress swinging above beautiful shapely legs.

NEW WAY TO FLY

AMANDA DROVE through the city streets toward her apartment. She arched her shoulders wearily and frowned at the lights of Brock Munroe's truck in the rearview mirror, wondering what had possessed her to invite him back to her place for a drink.

Not that she hadn't enjoyed the evening. In fact, she'd been surprised by the ease and warmth of their dinner conversation, and by how interesting the man actually was when you managed to get past his rough cowboy exterior.

Amanda moved restlessly in the driver's seat, troubled by a random memory of what it was like to dine out with Edward. She recalled his subtle witty stories and brittle jokes, usually at other people's expense, interspersed with long awkward silences while Amanda searched her mind for something to say, anything that he might find entertaining.

She hadn't felt that way at all with Brock Munroe. During the whole evening, she'd had the pleasant sensation that she was bright and fascinating, a beautiful woman with an impressive mind and all kinds of positive attributes.

It *did* feel good for a change, Amanda told herself with a wry private grin, to spend time with somebody who thought you were wonderful. It did wonders for your self-esteem.

Amanda pulled up in front of her building and waved an arm to indicate the visitor parking, then ducked into her own reserved space. She sat behind the wheel for a moment, thinking about the man she'd just spent the evening with.

He was far more complex than she'd given him credit for, this Brock Munroe. He presented a cheerful disheveled appearance, but he was no fool. And he might have given Amanda all kinds of praise, but she suspected that deep down, he wasn't really convinced of her value or her sincerity.

"So who cares?" Amanda muttered aloud, gathering up her handbag and gloves with an abrupt angry gesture. "Who the hell cares one bit what Brock Munroe thinks? I'll never see him again, after I get this evening over with."

She met him in the lobby with a cool gracious smile, rode silently up to her floor and unlocked her apartment. She glanced at him critically as she opened the door. He'd obviously spruced up a bit for this date, put on a pair of dark tan jeans and a crisply ironed cream-colored shirt under his brown leather jacket. The Western cut of the clothes flattered his wonderful physique, showing to fine advantage the broad shoulders and lean hips, the long muscular thighs that felt like iron when she brushed against him inadvertently as they entered the foyer together.

Still, she had to suppress a little shudder of alarm when she imagined Edward meeting this man, and thought about what Edward would probably say later on the subject of Brock Munroe.

"Who *was* that masked man?" she heard him asking in his flat nasal imitation of a Texas drawl. "Say, did anybody get the number of his horse? Does he wear those boots to bed, d'you think?"

Amanda shook off the mental image and gave Brock a brief automatic smile, hanging his leather jacket in the closet while he stood gazing at her apartment in silence.

She was conscious of a sudden heaviness in the air, of a growing discomfort and annoyance.

Brock hated her apartment.

She could tell just by the set of his shoulders, the sudden tension in his brown hands, the guarded look in his dark eyes when he turned to her.

Don't say it, Amanda warned him silently, indicating the leather sofa and moving gracefully through the room toward the kitchen. *Don't you dare say what you're thinking, because I can't bear to hear it, and I'll just . . .*

"Would you like a mixed drink, or a glass of wine?" she asked, pausing in front of her small black-lacquered china cabinet.

"Do you have Scotch?"

"Almost a whole bottle. I don't drink Scotch very often."

"That's fine, then. A little Scotch on the rocks, please, with just a touch of soda."

Amanda nodded, took a heavy crystal tumbler and a wineglass from the cabinet and vanished into the kitchen. She mixed his drink with trembling hands, painfully conscious of him sitting there in her living room, looking around at the elegant decor and forming judgments.

And why did his judgments matter to her so much anyhow? She'd already dismissed the man as being of little consequence, impossibly far away from her in matters of sophistication and taste. Brock Munroe was nothing to her but a passing acquaintance, a friend of a friend.

So why did it cause her such embarrassment to sense his silent criticism? Why did she hate the idea that he was looking at her apartment and her life with wry humor and private scorn?

Amanda put the ice cube tray back in the fridge, pausing to press her hands to her hot flushed cheeks for a moment.

Finally, her composure somewhat restored, she carried the drinks into the living room, set them on the glass coffee table and sank into a black sling chair opposite Brock.

"So," she inquired with a challenging glance, "what do you think of my New York look?"

"I hate it," he said quietly, reaching for the drink. "Don't you?"

Amanda stared at him, aghast at his rudeness. Her cheeks turned pale and her blue eyes flashed dangerously. "Of course I don't hate it," she said evenly. "I chose this decor myself, and put a lot of time and thought into it.''

Brock leaned back on the couch and sipped his drink, gazing at her steadily over the rim of his glass. ''That's not what I mean,'' he said finally. ''I suppose it's stylish as hell, and it shows that you're first-rate at what you do, and all that. But when I look at something like this, I always wonder if people really *like* it, or of it's just done for effect. I mean,'' he added reasonably, waving an arm to take in the quiet room around them, ''how could anybody possibly like this?''

''Let me get this straight,'' Amanda said, so angry that she could hardly control herself. ''You're accusing me of hypocrisy, is that it, Brock? Of creating a certain look just to impress other people at the expense of my own preference?''

Brock considered this, his dark eyes calm as he looked around at the wrought iron and glass, the cold abstract atmosphere of the place, the stark monochrome color scheme. His eyes rested briefly on the only painting in the room, a huge modernist work above the dining table that featured two broad intersecting red lines on a field of pale gray.

The purchase of this painting, by one of Edward's favorite artists, had cleaned out most of Amanda's savings. She tensed as Brock raised a cynical dark eyebrow, almost ready to strike the man if he made some disparaging comment. But he didn't, just nodded and turned back to her with an easy smile.

"Yeah," he drawled. "I guess that's what I'm saying, Amanda."

"I beg your pardon?"

"That's what I'm saying. I think this place…" He paused to wave a hand once more to include everything in the room. "I think this is a form of hypocrisy, if that's how you want to put it. I don't think it's really your own taste. I'd say you've done it just for effect."

"Oh, really? And what do you know about my taste?" Amanda asked him in low furious tones. "What do you know about me at all? We exchanged a few words at a party and had dinner together once. Does that make you some kind of expert on me?"

"No," he said quietly. "Of course it doesn't. But I was attracted to you the minute I laid eyes on you, Amanda Walker. I thought you were the most beautiful woman I've ever seen, and I also thought there was more to you than a few inches of style and glamour. Fact is, I still do. After all, how could I have been so wrong for all those years?"

"What do you mean, all those years?"

With a sudden uncomfortable shrug he drained his glass, set it down on the table and got to his feet. "Forget it," he said abruptly. "I meant something else. Thanks for the nice evening, Amanda," he added with formal politeness, extending his hand. "It was a real pleasure."

Still shaken by their exchange, she took his hand briefly and was once again almost overwhelmed by the firmness of his grip, by the feel of his warm flesh against hers and the dark compelling depths of his eyes as he gazed down at her.

"Thank you," she murmured, struggling to compose herself, to keep her voice light and casual. "Let's just put all this behind us and consider the issue closed, all right?"

"Sure," Brock said easily, moving toward the closet to get his jacket. "All in the past, Amanda. And I won't be bothering you again. But the invitation's still open if you feel like dropping in someday to give me advice about my house."

Amanda stared at him, caught off guard by his words. "You're kidding," she said with forced lightness. "You haven't exactly been bowled over by my decorating, Brock. So why on earth would you want advice from someone like me?"

"You don't understand. I don't like this place, Amanda, not one bit. But that doesn't change anything. I still happen to believe that your advice would be real valuable."

She shifted nervously, confused by the conflicting messages his words contained. "Maybe it's best just to let it go, Brock," she said finally. "But thanks for the vote of confidence, if that's what it is."

He opened the door and turned to give her one more thoughtful glance, hesitating as if on the verge of saying something else. Then he was gone, striding off toward the elevator, his tall figure looking vital and larger than life in the silent polished confines of the apartment hallway.

Long after he disappeared around the corner, Amanda stood gazing blankly in the direction he'd vanished, her eyes bleak, her face distant and sad.

When she finally went back into her apartment the place looked much less satisfying than it had just a day earlier. The stark walls and furnishings seemed almost to be mocking her, chilly and silent, devoid of comfort, so lonely all at once that she was tempted to sink down on the cold leather couch and cry like a lost child.

MARY GIBSON STOOD in a cramped dingy washroom behind the service station, arching her back and trying to see more of herself in the cloudy mirror. Nervously she rummaged in her handbag, put on some lipstick, frowned and smudged most of it off again, then tried once more to catch a full-length glimpse of herself.

Mary knew that she looked nice. She wore the beautifully fitted gray flannel trousers and soft sea-blue sweater that she'd bought from Amanda Walker, and they flattered her more than any clothes she'd ever owned. And her hair was trimmed and shaped, tinted a dark ash blond with sunny highlights that softened her face and deepened the golden brown of her eyes.

She wore a little makeup, too, applied with a spare skillful hand the way Amanda had shown her. It was surprising what a difference that made, just a tiny bit of color and contouring. Mary felt confident about her appearance, but not about what she was about to do. In fact, this was one of the hardest things she'd ever done in her life.

Slowly, her face set and grim, Mary took her handbag and cast one final look at her reflection in the mirror. Then she went out, climbed into her waiting car and drove the last few miles.

She pulled up a long curving drive and through the electronic gates in the direction of a low complex built of gray cinder block. When the buildings were directly in front of her, Mary almost changed her mind. It took all her strength of will not to put her car in reverse, turn around and roar off through the gates in the direction of home, away from all the terror and misery of this place.

The drive to the prison had seemed endless. She wondered why they had to put Al in a jail clear across the state. Maybe it had something to do with security, and the fact that most people wouldn't want a prison in their neighborhood. But then most people didn't have to visit their husbands in prison.

Mary wondered if anybody from Crystal Creek had made this long drive to visit *her* husband. Did Martin Avery or Vernon Trent or J.T. McKinney ever give up their weekends, get up before dawn to drive all this way?

Did Billie Jo Dumont?

Mary shivered suddenly and gripped the wheel, almost blinded by emotion. She parked in the lot and got out, moving with halting steps toward the marked doors at the front of the complex.

If anybody from Crystal Creek had come to visit, they'd never talked to Mary about it. Of course, she reflected, they never talked about her husband at all. The whole town maintained a kind of tactful silence about Al in her presence, as if he'd died suddenly and she needed to be protected from the pain of his memory.

That would have been so much easier to bear, Mary told herself miserably, presenting her visitor's card and submitting to a cursory search by the female admitting guard. If her husband had died, she'd have all the dignity and respect of a widow in the community. Instead, she was a sort of outcast, an embarrassment to everyone who met her.

Not that Mary didn't understand their discomfort. After all, what could you say to a woman whose husband had cheated on her openly with a girl young enough to be their daughter, then went to jail for insurance fraud? No wonder they were all embarrassed by her.

Mary lifted her chin and bit her lip to prevent herself from crying. She followed the signs to a large room with stained pale green walls, filled with little wooden tables and shabby folding chairs.

People sat at most of the tables, men in faded blue institutional pants and shirts, women of all ages. Some of the couples were holding hands, gazing at each other while one or both of them cried silently. Others talked in earnest murmurs and a few were arguing in low tones.

Mary gave her card to an official, then seated herself at one of the empty tables and waited, balling a tissue tight in her hand and gripping it frantically.

She saw Al come through a door on the other side of the room. He stood looking around while Mary gazed at him, forgetting her own discomfort, stunned by his appearance.

Al "Bubba" Gibson had always been a substantial man, with an impressive breadth of shoulder on a heavy six-foot frame. In recent years, he'd even run a little to fat, carrying a rounded arrogant belly above his jeans like a trophy.

But all that was changed now. In the weeks since Mary had last seen her husband he appeared to have shrunk. The cheap blue cotton pants and shirt hung limply on him, making him seem stooped and old.

There was a lot more gray in his thick shaggy hair, and his face had an unhealthy pallor.

Of course, this was the first time she'd ever seen Al without a tan. Even in Mary's earliest memories his skin had always had a weathered warm look, with deep laughter lines in his cheeks and little wrinkles next to those sparkling blue eyes. . . .

Suddenly she felt a wave of pain, of loss and sorrow so shattering that it was all she could do to keep from moaning aloud and hurrying out of the room.

But it was too late. Al had seen her, and was moving awkwardly though the crowded room in her direction.

Finally he stopped by Mary's table, gazed at her for a long tense moment, then began to look around for a chair.

"Here, Al," Mary said quickly, getting up and pulling an empty chair from an adjoining table, carrying it around to him. "Here's a chair."

He took it, still silent, gazing at his wife in stunned astonishment. "Mary. . ." he began. His voice cracked and he paused, trying to smile at her. "You sure do look nice, girl. Real nice."

The ghost of that old cheerful smile brought fresh tears to her eyes. Once again she fought to compose herself. "Thanks, Al," she said finally. "I just got my hair done on Friday. And I bought some new clothes the other day, too."

"Well, good for you," he said warmly. "I'm real glad to hear it."

Mary swallowed hard and seated herself opposite him, knowing that what he said was true. Al had always been a generous husband. He liked Mary to dress well, and frequently during their married life he'd tried to coax her to fix herself up, spend a little money on her hair and wardrobe.

Maybe I should have listened to him, Mary thought bleakly. *Maybe if I'd taken better care of myself, he wouldn't have had to . . .*

"I just can't get over it," Al went on, smiling shyly across the table. "You really do look pretty, Mary. You're a sight for sore eyes."

"Oh, Al . . ." This time it was Mary's turn to fall abruptly silent, not trusting her voice. "Do you see anybody else?" she asked finally. "Do folks come to visit you, Al?"

He shook his head. "Not much. It's a long drive, Mary, an' they're all busy with their own lives. Martin an' Vern drove up one day just after I came here, but Vern's married now, an' Martin's busy all the time. You know how it is for folks."

Mary nodded. "How about J.T.?"

"He came a couple times, back earlier on, at the very beginning, but now that Cynthia's so close to her time, he don't like to leave her alone that much."

Mary hesitated, gripping the tissue so tightly in her fist that her fingernails dug into her callused palm. But she had to ask. "And... and Billie Jo?"

Al's face twisted in pain, and his blue eyes clouded. "Mary, that's all over. It was over before this happened, even. I was just crazy for a while there, I guess," he concluded simply. "I can't think of no other explanation."

Mary nodded. She gazed at her husband, searching inside herself for the old bracing anger, but it seemed to be gone. All she felt was sorrow for what they'd lost, and an aching flood of pity for the pale shrunken man across from her.

"I guess you were," she said finally. "But you're paying an awful price for it, aren't you, Al? Just awful."

"I sure am," he said without emotion. "I'm livin' in hell, an' I'll be here for another two years. Does that make you happy, Mary?"

She shook her head. "Not a bit," she said truthfully. "Not one bit, Al. It makes me sad."

Her husband lifted his haggard face and gazed at her with a flare of emotion in those tired blue eyes. "You always were a strange one, Mary," he said with an attempt at a smile. "After what I put you through, most women would just be laughin' to see that I got what I deserved."

"There's nothing funny about this," Mary said. "Not for any of us."

"It's real bad, isn't it?" he asked after another awkward silence. "The ranch an' all. There's just no money, is there?"

Mary shook her head.

"That's why I wrote an' asked you to come up, Mary," Al said finally. "I want you to go ahead an' sell. Get Vern to fax the real estate papers up to the prison office here so I can sign the forms, okay?"

Mary stared at him, stunned. "Al..." she whispered. "Al, what are you saying? You want to sell the *ranch?*"

He shifted restlessly on the hard wooden chair. "Hell, Mary, what else can we do? You're entitled to half of what we've got, but the only money's in the land. An' I can't hardly mortgage it while I'm in prison, can I? How am I gonna make mortgage payments from a jail cell? So you go ahead an' file for divorce, an' we'll sell the ranch so you can get your money."

She stared at him blankly. "Divorce?"

Al returned her gaze. "Divorce, Mary," he said gently. "You got all the grounds in the world. Just go ahead. I'm not gonna put up any fight. You can get rid of me an' have some security for yourself. God knows you deserve it, after all these years. Maybe," he added wistfully, "after the ranch sells, you'd wanna go up an' live in Connecticut somewhere, close to Sara an' the grandkids. Wouldn't that be nice, Mary?"

Mary licked her lips, still gazing blankly at him. "But...but what about you?" she whispered finally. "After you...after you get out? I can't picture you living anywhere but right there on that ranch, Al. Why, you were born there, and so was your father."

"An' my grandfather," he added quietly. "But those ol' boys, they were better men than me, Mary. I guess the Gibson family had to run aground sometime, an' I sure did it up with a bang, didn't I?"

Mary shivered at the self-hatred in his voice. "You made some mistakes, Al," she said quietly. "God knows, we all make mistakes in our lives. I think that spending two years in here is enough of a price to pay. I don't think you should lose your ranch. And I don't know if I'm ready to think about divorce right now, either."

Al stared at her, his eyes darkening suddenly with emotion. "What're you tellin' me, Mary?" he whispered, his voice husky. "Are you sayin' you still...you still want me?"

Mary shook her head. "I don't know, Al," she said honestly. "You hurt me real bad, and I won't deny it. Maybe you even killed any feelings I could have for you anymore. But I still need some more time to think about things. I don't want other people making my decisions anymore. And I sure don't want to sell the ranch if we can hold on to it."

"Mary...oh, God, girl..." He reached across and grasped her hand, his big shoulders heaving as he struggled to regain control of himself.

Mary squeezed his hand, then extricated her own gently. "But it's not going to be easy, Al," she said in a businesslike tone. "There's all those bank loans, and Cody Hendricks says we've got to start showing a strong profit before he can give us a new line of credit for operating capital."

"Pretty tough to show a strong profit with beef prices at an all-time low," Al said bitterly.

"That's what I told him. But Cody's got a point, too, Al. He's the bank manager, and he's got his own job to think about. He can't keep carrying the Flying Horse at a loss to the bank."

Al gave her another ghost of that old cheerful grin. "Imagine my little Mary talkin' to bank managers about profit margins an' operatin' capital."

Mary flushed under his warm admiring gaze. "We do what we have to," she said briefly.

"Does Cody have any ideas?"

Mary shook her head. "Not really. But he's given me some time to work things out, as long as I sell the calves next week and buy down the interest on the loans. And I keep thinking there's an idea somewhere...something at the back of my mind that would solve all these problems if I could just manage to grab on to it..."

Al shook his head sadly. "That'd be real nice, girl, but those things are usually just dreams. In real life, problems don't tend to get solved that easy."

Mary nodded, accepting the truth of his words.

"What's the weather been like?" her husband asked shyly. "Is it gettin' real cool an' crisp in the mornin's, these days?"

Mary's heart ached for him all over again. She looked into his face, seeing the hunger in his eyes for news of home, of the rolling green acres that he loved.

Finally she swallowed the lump in her throat, gripped his hand again and began talking. "It's real nice, Al. The calves are looking good, and you know what? That bay mare, Sunshine, she surprised us all by dropping a little pinto colt just last week. Even Manny was shocked."

"No kiddin'!" he said, his eyes lighting. "Can you imagine that? I never even knew she was in foal."

For a long time they talked, and their words carried both of them away from the drab room and its sad occupants, into the sun-washed past and far away to a green and silent place that existed only in their memories and their dreams.

CHAPTER SEVEN

AMANDA DROVE along a tree-lined country lane, gazing with concern at the billowing gray clouds drifting above a distant line of hills. The afternoon was dark and leaden, heavy with the threat of rain and a brooding gloomy atmosphere that reflected her despondent mood.

Of course, her despondency had little to do with the weather. Amanda was tense and edgy these days, filled with enough self-doubt to cloud even the brightest day.

Much of her unhappiness sprang from her relationship with Edward, who had arrived several days ago and didn't seem in any hurry to leave. In fact, Amanda could not recall Edward Price ever being so relaxed and patient, so obviously willing to wait for what he wanted.

And he was leaving no doubt at all that he wanted Amanda. She knew him well enough to realize that he'd embarked on this mission with all of his customary single-minded ambition, and he hadn't the slightest intention of taking no for an answer. Although Edward seemed easygoing and calm, in a placid holiday mood, Amanda sensed that this was just another part of his overall game plan.

They knew each other so well, Amanda thought ruefully, watching as a couple of heavy raindrops splattered against her windshield.

She knew exactly what Edward was thinking and planning almost all the time. On the other hand, he also understood her well enough not to press, to be sociable and casual while tempting her with offhand remarks about the luxurious condo he planned to buy in New York, the high-powered job he was prepared to offer her, the trips they'd take to Rome and Paris to review the latest fashions.

And there was no doubt that Amanda was tempted.

There was something familiar, predictable and reassuring about Edward. With him, Amanda slipped back into their old relationship of mentor and protégé, discovering with relief that she could still make him laugh. She entertained him with pointed witty stories about her clients, delighting him with her sophistication and the brittle charm she'd cultivated so well.

But she was also troubled by something that seemed to be lacking in their new relationship, some essential ingredient that had once sparkled and danced between them, charging the very air with excitement and sexual tension. Amanda missed that volatile feeling of promise and breathless abandon.

But then, she and Edward still weren't sleeping together, and that made such a big difference....

Amanda's forehead creased and a small pucker formed between her brows. She skimmed past the gate to Brock Munroe's property, annoyed by the warm flush that touched her cheeks and prickled at her throat when she remembered her unsettling evening with the rancher, the astounding things he'd said and the anger she'd felt.

At least Edward was a better companion than *that* oaf, Amanda told herself scornfully.

Edward Price would never tell people bluntly that he hated their apartment. Instead, he'd praise them with a few gracious, well-chosen words, making them feel like the most talented decorators in the world. Then, when they were safely out of earshot, he'd jeer to his companions about the tacky decor, making everybody laugh with brilliant barbed witticisms at his hosts' expense.

Amanda gripped the wheel, suddenly chilled by her thoughts of Edward and the way he treated people. Strangely, these things had never bothered her before because he was so exquisitely polite, so beautifully well-mannered that he never insulted anyone openly, never made them feel less than wholly welcome and admired.

Only those who were close to Edward Price knew what he really thought about people. Amanda had always been so tremendously flattered to be one of Edward's intimates, to be the person in whom he confided most of his feelings and opinions.

But now, for some reason, she found that she wasn't nearly as thrilled by Edward's intimacy and his confidences. In fact, a lot of the time she was downright irritated by him, and often surprised him with the sudden coldness in her eyes, the tart edge to her voice when she answered some sarcastic remark.

Amanda slowed for the gate to the Flying Horse, Mary Gibson's ranch, still brooding over Edward and the surprising new complexity of their relationship.

The problem, she decided, was that she hadn't yet invited him back into her bed. That simple fact was no doubt the source of all the tension and edginess that she felt between them.

Edward was absolutely right, Amanda told herself. She was being silly about the whole thing. Why not just relieve their mutual pressure by going to bed with the man? After all, she'd lived with him for almost four years, and she hadn't been with anyone else since she left him six months ago.

No wonder she was feeling so ragged and fragile....

Tonight would be different, Amanda decided with sudden firmness, pulling up and parking by Mary

Gibson's ranch house just as the heavens opened and the rain began to pour down.

She'd go to bed with Edward tonight. Better yet, she'd invite him to leave the hotel, move his things over to her place for the rest of his visit, see if they could recapture the wonderful feelings they'd once had when they shared an apartment and a bed.

The decision made her feel better immediately. By the time she gathered her pink-striped packages from the back seat and sprinted up the walk toward the kitchen door she was laughing, shaking raindrops from her dark hair when Mary answered the doorbell.

"Hi, Mary," Amanda said, giving the other woman a hug and following her into the big ranch kitchen. "My goodness, it's pouring out there. I almost—"

Her smile faded and she fell abruptly silent, looking at Luke Harte, who lounged casually by the table, booted feet extended, denim jacket hung on a chair back. He nursed a mug of coffee and looked up at her without smiling.

"Hi, Luke," Amanda said, feeling awkward. "Having a coffee break?"

The young man's dark eyes moved over her face and body with a slow intent gaze that fell just short of being insolent.

"Just visitin' with Mary," he said in his quiet cowboy drawl. "She gets real lonesome in here by herself all day long."

"I suppose she does," Amanda said, still unnerved by his steady gaze. "But," she added with forced cheerfulness, "I've brought some entertainment for her. I finally found that gray silk blouse, Mary," she added, turning to the woman who stood by the counter piling donuts onto an oval dish. "And another one, too, that I thought you might like, and the rust-colored jumpsuit I told you about last week."

Mary's eyes brightened. "Oh, good," she said with childlike enthusiasm. "Amanda, I'm getting to be such a clotheshorse. I love this stuff."

Luke got to his feet and shrugged into his jacket. "See you, Mary," he said over his shoulder as he ambled to the door. "I'm workin' on that truck some more. I'll be right outside in the garage if you need me," he added pointedly with a glance in Amanda's direction.

"Oh, don't worry, Luke," Amanda said, struggling to make her voice light and joking. "I'm sure Mary will be all right. It's been weeks and weeks since I attacked anybody in their own kitchen."

Luke said nothing, just looked at Amanda coolly for a moment before he opened the door and stepped out into the driving rain.

Mary seemed unaware of the sudden tension in the room. She was setting out a mug for Amanda, along with cream and sugar and the fragrant plate of fresh sugar donuts.

"Mary, you'll make me fat," Amanda protested laughingly. "You're such a good cook, and I always eat like a pig when I have a chance to get these home-baked things."

"I wish you'd come for a meal sometime," Mary said shyly. "If you think my *baking's* good, you should taste my barbecued brisket."

"I can just imagine," Amanda said wistfully. But she was chilled by the mental image of herself and Mary eating together, with Luke Harte's watchful dark face across the table. . . .

"So, Mary," she said, sitting down and reaching gratefully for the steaming coffee mug. "What's been happening with you lately?"

"Well, I went to see Al on the weekend," Mary began, flushing slightly, her obvious tension belying the casualness of the words.

"Really? How was he?"

"He was real sad," Mary said quietly. "Not at all like he used to be. It must be so hard, being locked away in a place like that."

Amanda shivered at the thought. "Oh, Mary," she said impulsively, clasping the older woman's hand and squeezing it gently, "it must have been hard for you, too."

"It was." Mary fell silent for a moment, then continued. "Al wants to sell the ranch. He says we should get a divorce, sell the ranch and split up the money so I can have my share. He thinks I should go up to Connecticut, find a place to live somewhere close to my daughter and her family."

Amanda stirred her coffee nervously, wondering what to say. "How about you?" she asked. "Is that what you want, Mary?"

Mary shrugged and got up, moving across the room to pick a couple of dead leaves from a geranium in a yellow pot on the windowsill. "I don't know what I want," she said without turning around. "Sometimes I think it'd be so nice just to get away from all these problems, but other times..."

"Other times?" Amanda prompted gently.

"I don't know," Mary said again, returning to her chair. "Anyhow," she added with an attempt at a smile, "I likely don't have any choice. If I don't come up with an idea soon to make some money on this place, we'll have to sell it to satisfy the bank. So it'll be out of my hands anyway."

"Oh, Mary..." Amanda began.

Mary shook her head and made another attempt to smile. "Well, that's enough about me," she said, adding, "I stopped at Brock's place yesterday."

Amanda paused halfway through the donut and looked up, her mouth full, blue eyes questioning.

"Poor Brock," Mary said, not noticing Amanda's reaction. "He's in such a mess. He's renovating his house, you know."

"I know. He mentioned it to me."

"Well, he sure could use some help. The poor boy, he's done a beautiful job so far, but he's got to make some decisions about decorating now, and I think he's stuck."

Amanda felt a treacherous stirring of interest. "What's his house like?" she asked.

"Oh, the Munroe place is a beautiful old house. Caspar Munroe—he was Brock's great-grandfather—built that house more than eighty years ago, and he didn't spare any expense, believe me."

"Two-storey?" Amanda asked wistfully. "One of those that's all made of stone, with an upper balcony?"

Mary nodded. "And a long shady front veranda with big pillars, and all kinds of golden oak inside, wainscoting and plate rails, staircases and newel posts, and wide, wide door moldings..."

Amanda stared dreamily off into space. "Hardwood floors?"

"Every room. And a huge fieldstone fireplace, big enough to roast a steer in, and lovely crystal chandeliers that were shipped down from St. Louis, piece by piece, before World War I..."

"Oh, God," Amanda said, shivering. "What's he doing to it?" she asked abruptly. "What kind of renovations, Mary?"

"Well, the place has gotten pretty run-down over the years. I think Brock's putting in a whole new kitchen and replacing a lot of the old lath and plaster that's falling to pieces. And the heating system, too, I believe. Most of that's done already. But now he has to decide if he's going to..."

"You know, I just *hate* this kind of thing!" Amanda interrupted, her eyes dark with emotion. "I can't bear the way people modernize and destroy the ambience of those gorgeous old houses. There ought to be some kind of law."

"Oh, I don't think Brock's destroying his house," Mary said mildly. "He's doing a real nice job, actually. He's just not sure about wallpaper designs and cupboards, that sort of thing."

"He shouldn't try to make anything look too modern," Amanda said firmly. "He should be upgrading while retaining the period atmosphere."

"Well now, maybe you should stop in and tell him that," Mary suggested, glancing up at Amanda's flashing blue eyes.

Amanda hesitated, then nodded, sipping her coffee thoughtfully. "I think I will," she said. "After we get finished, Mary, I think I just might drop in there on my way home and see what he's doing."

"Good idea. Like I said, he could sure use the help. But I've got you first," Mary added cheerfully, pouring more coffee into Amanda's mug. "I can't wait to see that jumpsuit. I've never worn a jumpsuit."

Amanda smiled fondly at the other woman. They lingered at the kitchen table, sipping coffee and chatting about clothes while the rain pounded against the windows. But Amanda's eyes were distant and preoccupied, and part of her thoughts were clearly elsewhere.

BROCK PUT HIS HAMMER in the little pocket on his carpenter's apron and frowned at the section of baseboard he'd just replaced. Alvin sat beside him, sniffing contemptuously at the new wood.

"Oh, come on, Alvin," Brock said cheerfully. "Don't keep acting like that. I shaped that piece of oak so nice that you can't even tell which part is old and which is new. Don't be so damn critical."

Alvin gave his master a cold look of disdain and wandered off toward the kitchen, sniffing hopefully under the table and around the bottom of the fridge.

He paused by the door and gave a couple of lazy barks, then glanced expectantly through the archway at Brock, who still knelt by his new baseboard, running a hand over the beautifully fitted section of oak.

"No way, Alvin," Brock muttered without looking up. "I let you out just twenty minutes ago, you monster. You'll just run around outside and then track mud all over the new hardwood floor."

Alvin barked again, with slightly more energy, and Brock shrugged, bending to peer at a miter joint that was a shade off perfection.

"What's the matter? You *know* you don't want to go outside. There's still some thunder out there, you little coward, and you're scared to death of thunder."

"No, I'm not," Alvin said in a hauntingly familiar voice, causing Brock to stiffen and leap to his feet, gazing wildly into the kitchen.

Amanda Walker stood there in a stylish pale green rain cape, with water droplets glistening like showers of diamonds on her shining dark curls.

Brock was so astounded at this apparition that he gaped, stunned speechlessly by her loveliness. The woman glowed like a candle in the shadowed depths of his big untidy kitchen, her cheeks pink, her blue eyes shining like stars. To Brock, she looked like a flower, all cream and pink and blue, rising from a chrysalis of green in some warm spring rain.

"I knocked twice," she said at last, shifting uncomfortably under his intense gaze. "Nobody answered."

"Sorry," he muttered. "It's . . . I guess it's raining so hard, and I was . . . I was talking to Alvin."

Amanda grinned, then looked down to hide her smile. "I see," she murmured solemnly. "And this big fellow is Alvin, I take it?"

After a brief but careful appraisal, Alvin had obviously fallen in love. He crept across the room and dropped himself humbly at Amanda's feet, then rolled over onto his back, waving his paws and exposing his fat belly.

Amanda bent to tickle his silky abdomen and Alvin grunted, eyes closed in bliss, legs moving in rhythmic shivers of ecstasy.

"Yeah, that's Alvin," Brock said grimly, watching with envy while Amanda knelt close to the prostrate fat dog and caressed him, murmuring endearments. "He's just a big phony, you know," Brock felt compelled to add. "He's not usually this nice. He's only doing it to impress you."

"Putting on the dog, you mean?" Amanda asked, with a sparkling glance up at the tall man who stood in the archway.

Brock chuckled and moved closer, reaching down to help her to her feet. "Let me take that wet thing," he said, indicating her elegant cape. "To what do I owe the honor of this visit, Miss Walker?"

"Oh, your house *is* lovely," Amanda breathed, letting him remove the cape from her shoulders and gazing around at the big square rooms. "I was just over at Mary's and she tried to describe it, but I don't think I've ever seen woodwork this beautiful. Look at it! This is solid oak, all of it.''

"Yeah, I know it is," Brock said dryly, spreading the cape carefully across a gleaming old ladder-back chair that stood nearby. "And after all these years, it's just as dry and hard as rock. You should see how many saw blades I've dulled since I've been working on this stuff.''

Amanda stared up at him in alarm. "You're not *cutting* any of this wood, are you?''

Brock shrugged and took off his carpenter's apron, tossing it onto a pile of paint tins in the hallway. "I don't like to," he said, "but sometimes it's necessary. I have to replace some damaged parts and have to make a splice. This doorframe, for instance," he added casually, glancing down at Amanda. "Can you tell what part's new, and what's eighty years old?''

Amanda looked at him cautiously, then turned to the wooden moulding, running a hand over its gleaming surface. "You're kidding me, Brock," she said finally. "You can't possibly have replaced any of this. It's all original."

Brock shook his head, obviously delighted by her reaction. "See the lintel?" he said, reaching up to touch the ornate carved wood. "That was shattered forty years ago when my granddaddy accidentally fired off a shotgun blast in the kitchen. The whole piece was split and broken, so I took it off and used it as a model to make a new one.''

Amanda gazed at him, wide-eyed, then looked back up at the piece of oak that topped the doorframe. ''But it's perfect!'' she said in amazement. ''It's the same pattern, the same color, everything.''

''I used four or five different router blades to shape the molding,'' Brock told her calmly. ''And I experimented with about a dozen kinds of stain before I found one that was exactly right.''

Amanda nodded thoughtfully, looking up again at the beautiful carved molding. Then she moved through into the big living room, pausing to peer closely at the side of the archway. ''Pocket doors?'' she asked, glancing over her shoulder at Brock.

He nodded. ''Two of 'em. Solid oak, all beveled panels, and four feet wide each.''

''Oh, my,'' Amanda breathed. ''May I see them?''

Brock shook his head. ''They won't slide out because the track's warped. That's my next project, to get the doors running smooth. But after that,'' he added gloomily, ''I don't know what I can do. I'm stuck.''

Amanda glanced back through the arched doorway at Brock's kitchen, where cupboards had been removed from the walls and dishes and packages of food were lying around in cardboard boxes, on open shelves, on the floor.

"It looks like there's all kinds of work to do," she ventured.

"Oh, no doubt of that," Brock said grimly. "I just don't know where to start. I'm scared to make mistakes, Amanda. This kitchen was built in the days when they still got their water supply from a hand pump connected to a storage tank. I don't know what kind of design would fit in and be efficient without spoiling the atmosphere, you know?"

Amanda nodded approval at that. She reached over and patted his arm. Brock's body shuddered at the casual touch.

"That's just the way you should be thinking," she said, apparently unaware of his powerful reaction to her nearness. "It's such a big responsibility, renovating and preserving one of these lovely old houses. It certainly shouldn't be approached carelessly."

As she spoke, Amanda strolled back into the kitchen and looked around, frowning intently.

Brock followed her, seeing the room through her eyes. "Sorry about this awful mess," he muttered with some embarrassment. "Seems like I just never get a chance to—"

"Don't be silly," Amanda said briskly. "I know what it's like to renovate. Brock, I think glass-fronted cabinets would be perfect in here," she added, her eyes narrowing as she gazed around. "And I don't think they should be natural wood, either. People never used stained wood for cupboards back in those days."

"Painted?" Brock asked with sudden interest. "You think I should just use construction-grade wood and paint it?"

Amanda nodded. "I think a light cream enamel, with paneled glass doors."

Brock stared at her. "Yeah," he said with rising excitement. "I see what you mean, Amanda. That would brighten the whole room and look real authentic besides. It'd be a lot cheaper, too," he added cheerfully, "than buying a ton of oak or ash or something."

"Absolutely," Amanda said, catching his enthusiasm. "Oh, Brock, can't you just see this room with light cabinets, beveled glass doors, and this hardwood floor all finished with a dark stain, maybe partly covered with a braided rug?"

"I just laid that hardwood," Brock told her, hoping for more praise.

"Did you? Oh, my goodness, what a beautiful job! Brock, you do such lovely work," she exclaimed, kneeling to touch one of the perfect floor joints. Brock beamed at her, basking in her approval like a little boy.

"How about cupboard layout?" he asked, following her around, marveling at the way her unexpected arrival had somehow turned a dull rainy day into a little bit of heaven. "The sink used to be here, and the top cupboards were—"

"That's all wrong," Amanda said, waving a hand to cut him off. "You could fit in a small island on this side for more counter space, and it'd be much nicer to have the sink here under the window so you could use that wide sill for plants. There should be all kinds of plants in this kitchen, Brock. Hanging plants, ferns on antique stands...can't you just see it? Especially with glass-fronted cabinets!"

Brock thought this over. "Alvin would eat them," he said.

Amanda looked fondly down at the ugly dog who trailed close on her heels. "He would not," she protested. "*Would* you, Alvin?"

Alvin gazed up at her with a look of innocence, his pink tongue lolling, and licked her shoe humbly.

"Nice Alvin," Amanda crooned, bending to pat him and tickle his ears.

"Phony," Brock whispered furiously, following Amanda out of the room and giving Alvin a rude shove with his foot. "You big *phony*, Alvin."

Alvin gave his master a reproachful glance, then rushed across the room, plump body swaying, to catch up with Amanda. She stood by the vast fireplace, running her hands over the carved oak mantel.

"What are these initials?" she asked, gazing at a swirl of ornate lettering set in a wide oval on the expanse of golden oak.

"C.J.M. Caspar Josiah Munroe. My great-granddaddy carved that mantel with his own hands, the whole thing."

"Oh, it's just so lovely," Amanda whispered, touching the gleaming old wood with a reverent hand. "Brock, all these things are treasures. They're priceless. I wish I could..."

She fell silent abruptly, looking up at him, her eyes wide and startled.

"What, Amanda?" Brock asked gently, moving closer to her. "What do you wish?"

"Nothing," she said, shifting uncomfortably on her feet. "I just... I like this sort of thing so much. I wish I could do it myself."

"Carpentry?" Brock asked with a grin.

She smiled ruefully back at him. "Maybe not. I don't think I'd be all that skilled at the actual woodworking part. But I love getting an idea, you know, and then putting it into practice, taking something that's old and neglected and making it beautiful again."

"That's not what you told me that day I met you." Brock leaned an elbow against the mantel and looked down at her intently. She was standing so near that he could smell the damp fragrance of her hair and a faint elusive scent of perfume.

"It isn't?" She looked up at him with that same wide-eyed cautious look, almost a touch of shyness in her voice and face. But, Brock noticed, she made no effort to move away from him, to put distance between them.

"No," he said quietly. "Not at all. You said that you liked success, power, spending money, buying yourself beautiful clothes and cars and things like that."

Amanda flushed and shook her head. "I don't know why I said those things," she murmured, her voice so low that he had to strain to hear her. "I was...annoyed by you, and the way you acted, and I just...they're not really true, Brock."

"Then let's start again, shall we?" Brock whispered huskily. "Why don't you tell me what you're *really* like, girl?"

She placed her trembling hands on his broad chest as if to push him away. But Brock gathered her hands in both his own, then drew her tenderly into his arms and held her, shivering with the harsh agony of his longing.

"Oh, girl," he muttered into the fragrant tumble of her hair. "Amanda, I've dreamed about you all my life. Just you, sweetheart. Your eyes, your hair and face and smile..."

She shivered in his arms and he crushed her close to him, running his hands over her body, marveling at the beauty of her, the firm curving loveliness that felt so right in his arms.

She murmured something against his denim shirt-front and Brock bent to hear, but she looked up just then and their lips met, touched, melted together in a kiss that lasted forever, that left Brock shaken and dazed with a throbbing need to make love to this woman.

He began to move his hands more urgently and she finally pulled away, flushed and confused.

Brock sensed her agitation and dropped his hands, looking down at her gravely.

"I'm sorry, Amanda," he murmured, his voice husky with emotion. "I didn't mean to upset you. It's just that you're so..."

"Don't!" she whispered urgently, not looking at him. "Don't say it, Brock. Please," she added, glancing up at him with a pleading helpless expression that tore his heart. "Please, can't we both just forget this ever happened?"

"I can't," Brock said calmly. "Not as long as I live. But if that's what you want, Amanda, I won't mention it again, and it won't happen again unless you say so. I promise."

She nodded, looking down at the floor while he gazed at her dark glossy head.

"Would you like some coffee?" he asked after a moment's awkward silence.

She shook her head. "I just had some at Mary's. I have to get home," she added. "Edward will be waiting for me. We're going out to dinner."

"That's the New York boyfriend?" Brock asked, keeping his voice casual and turning away to hide the pain in his eyes.

"Yes. He's been here almost a week."

Brock gave her another intent glance. "I see. Well, I'd ask how you two are getting along, but it's none of my business, right?"

Amanda nodded uncertainly and moved with halting steps back into the kitchen, taking her cape from the chair and allowing Brock to help her put it on.

"Amanda," he said, pausing with his hands on her shoulders.

"Yes?"

"I meant what I said. Nothing like this will happen again unless you want it to. Do you believe me?"

She looked up at him, searching his face with eyes so blue and deep that Brock found himself in real danger of drowning. "Yes," she said finally, her voice grave and quiet. "Yes, Brock, I believe you."

"Good," he said, lifting his hands from her shoulders and trying to sound hearty. "In that case, do you think you could drop by again sometime soon, just to help me with the house? I told you before, Amanda, I really value your opinion, and I know you're interested in this kind of thing. We could work on it together as friends, no pressure of any kind. What about it?"

She paused and glanced wistfully around the littered old kitchen. "I'd like that," she said finally. "I'd really like that."

"That's great," Brock said briskly. "How about tomorrow?"

Amanda recoiled and moved nervously away. "Oh, no, not tomorrow," she whispered. "Tomorrow Edward and I are planning to...he's helping me with some inventory problems. I'm sorry, but I..."

"That's all right. Whenever you have the time, Amanda. I'm always here. Alvin, quit licking her shoes, you monster! She doesn't like you *that* much."

Amanda laughed, clearly relieved at the change of subject. "Alvin's a darling," she said, bending to caress the besotted little dog, who promptly rolled over again to present his abdomen.

Amanda patted him a few more times, then straightened, murmured something inaudible to Brock and hurried out to her car. Brock watched her running across his yard, a slim flash of pale green in the rain-washed landscape.

Long after her car disappeared from view, he stood in the kitchen doorway and gazed out into the flowing silver light, his face bleak with loneliness.

CHAPTER EIGHT

"I SUPPOSE you're going to be *far* too full for dessert," Edward said with an ironic grin, softening his words by reaching over to clasp Amanda's hand on the table.

"Yes, I probably am," Amanda said listlessly, causing her dinner companion to glance at her in surprise. "I wish I weren't," she added with a small faraway smile, freeing her hand and reaching for her wineglass. "This place serves the most wonderful chocolate cake."

She sipped her wine, unaware of Edward's concerned expression. Suddenly she was consumed by memories of Brock Munroe, of their dinner at this same restaurant, of his teasing conversation and his tanned quiet face in the candlelight.

And in spite of herself she remembered the way he'd kissed her just a few hours ago, an experience so shattering, so overpowering that she still quivered whenever she thought of his arms around her and his lips on hers.

Troubled and silent, Amanda picked at the remainder of her lobster and moved a piece of baked potato around on her plate.

What kind of woman was she, to be so completely absorbed with thoughts of one man while she was out with another? And far, far worse...what kind of woman would let a virtual stranger kiss her with that kind of passion on the very day she planned to invite another man into her bed?

The whole thing was just some bizarre physical attraction, Amanda told herself firmly. She and Brock Munroe were such total opposites that he fascinated her in a sort of dark subliminal way, and her only sane course of action was to avoid him altogether.

She certainly wasn't the first woman to have been confused by a pair of shoulders, by some man's finely molded lips and strong brown hands. But Amanda Walker was far too smart to let that kind of wayward sexual attraction spoil her whole life.

Amanda knew where she belonged. She knew what kind of life made her happy, and what kind of man she needed to be with, and she wasn't about to make any disastrous mistakes.

"Edward," she said abruptly, setting her fork down and gazing at the man across the table, "I've been thinking about...about us, and all the things you're offering me."

"Yes?" he said, his aquiline face suddenly cautious, his eyes guarded.

"And I think I've been acting a little silly since you got here, holding you at arm's length the way I have. Don't you?"

"I certainly do, Angel," he said, relaxing and raising his glass to her in a silent toast. "I most certainly do."

"Well, good," Amanda went on recklessly. "Actually, you know, I was thinking that tonight we should—"

"Anything else?" the waiter asked, materializing suddenly beside their table and stacking plates on his tray with silent efficiency.

Edward leaned back and gave the young man an expansive grin, the muted overhead light glinting on his well-barbered auburn head.

"Wal, Ah think we jest may be celebratin' somethin' heah," he said in a deliberate imitation of the waiter's warm Texas drawl. "Do y'all think y'all could brang us anothah bottle of thet wine?"

The young man stared down at him in silence for a long uncomfortable moment, then gave a brief clipped nod and disappeared with his tray full of used plates.

"Angel, why did he look so disapproving?" Edward asked, genuinely hurt. "I thought my accent was impeccable."

Amanda looked at him in amazement, overwhelmed by his thoughtless arrogance. "He knew you were making fun of him, Edward," she said coldly. "Besides," she added after a moment's awkward silence, "You used 'y'all' incorrectly."

"You mean there are grammatical rules?" Edward said with heavy irony, raising an elegant eyebrow. "Oh, do please enlighten me."

"It's plural," Amanda said firmly, ignoring his sarcastic tone. "'Y'all' refers to more than one person. For instance, if you meet a group of people you can say, 'How are y'all doing?' But you can't say it to just one person."

"I see." Edward paused, clearly on the verge of another jocular remark, but thought better of it when he saw Amanda's expression. "Sorry, Angel," he said contritely. "Correction accepted. I won't make the same mistake again, I promise. And I'll leave him a nice big tip to make up for my ignorance."

Amánda was silent, watching as the waiter delivered and uncorked their second bottle of wine.

"Apology accepted?" Edward prompted when they were alone, pouring the sparkling liquid into her tall crystal goblet.

"Yes, Edward," Amanda murmured. "And I'm sorry for being so sensitive. I didn't mean to jump on you."

"Sweetheart, you can jump on me any time you like," Edward told her with a warm significant smile. "In fact, you were saying...?"

Amanda looked at him, feeling strangely shy and awkward, wondering what to say. She still felt a sharp irritation with Edward because of his gaffe with the waiter.

But more than anything, Amanda also yearned for an end to the confusion in her mind, a return to a safe and comfortable world where events moved in predictable fashion from one point to the next.

For Amanda that world was with Edward, and always had been.

She swallowed hard and tried to smile at him. "I thought you might move your things over to my place tonight," she said softly. "I feel so lonely there, Edward."

"It's lonely in my hotel room, too, Angel. But I won't be coming tonight," he added, sipping casually at his wine.

"Why not?" Amanda gazed at him, stunned by this unexpected rejection.

Edward grinned and reached in his pocket for an envelope. "We're going to Dallas tonight, Angel," he told her. "Staying at the new convention center, attending the Southern Retailers' fall fashion show tomorrow. I have front row seats for both of us."

Amanda shook her head in confusion. "*Both* of us? At the Southern Retailers' show? Edward, those tickets have been sold out for months."

"Not if one knows the right people," Edward told her calmly. "I would have told you earlier, but I just confirmed the tickets this afternoon. And we're taking a local commuter flight that leaves at ten o'clock, so let's hurry home and pack your overnight bag, Angel. By the way," he added with a wolfish grin, "I hope you still have the pink silk negligee. That was always my personal favorite."

"But, Edward . . . I can't go to Dallas tonight."

"Why not? You told me you had a free day tomorrow, didn't you? It's going to be fabulous, Angel. There's a dealers' preshowing tomorrow afternoon, then cocktails and dinner and the first of the designers later in the evening."

"I know, but . . ." Amanda paused, biting her lip nervously. "Edward, the show is three days long. And I have a really heavy day on Thursday. I have to prepare for it tomorrow night. In fact, I'd have to come back right after the dealer showing."

"Don't be ridiculous," Edward said calmly, handing his credit card to the waiter without taking his eyes from Amanda's face. "You have to come and be available for all three days. This is an amazing opportunity, my dear. Contacts made at this show could be very, very valuable for us."

"Edward, I have four appointments on Thursday. Two of them are brand-new clients, both referred by friends. I have to—"

"Amanda, my sweet, aren't you forgetting something?" he murmured gently, reaching over and clasping her hand in both of his.

"What? What am I forgetting?"

"You just indicated that you've come to a decision about us, Angel. I gather you want to build a future with me. That means coming back to work with me in New York, and *that* means the end of this little business venture of yours. Doesn't it?"

Amanda was silent, gazing at the handsome man across the table in tense silence.

"I have no doubt it's been a valuable experience for you, and I truly have immense admiration for what you've managed to achieve," Edward told her with evident sincerity. "But your talents are needed elsewhere, darling. Just leave a sign on your office door canceling those appointments, or make a few calls from Dallas if you prefer the personal touch. But don't miss this opportunity."

Amanda shook her head. "I can't, Edward. It's my business. I can't just run off and dump clients like that."

"So what do you propose to do?" he asked mildly. "Continue servicing these clients of yours from a New York office after you move?"

"I just...I need a little more time," Amanda said. "If I'm going to close my business, I need time to do it properly."

"How much time?"

"I don't know the answer to that just yet," Amanda said. "But certainly more than a few hours."

"All right," he said cheerfully. They were silent while Edward escorted her from the restaurant, helped her with her coat, handed her courteously into the rental car he was using.

"Are you angry with me?" Amanda ventured, glancing over at his fine profile as he drove.

"Angry? Of course not. Just disappointed, Angel. And very, *very* sorry we couldn't get together tonight. It's been a long time, you know," Edward said with a brief smile. "Far too long."

Amanda nodded miserably. "I know."

She gazed out the window, brooding over how well Edward was apparently dealing with his disappointment.

There was no way you could really hurt Edward, she told herself. No matter what you said or did to him, he always seemed to walk away unscathed and cheerful, absorbed in his next project, barely aware of what you'd done.

Amanda suddenly found herself wondering if she really had been the primary reason for Edward's visit to Texas, or if he'd been planning all along to attend the Dallas show and she was just conveniently nearby.

But when he stopped in front of her apartment and turned to her with a meaningful smile, there was no doubting the sincerity in his gaze, or the naked sexual yearning when he touched her cheek and bent to kiss her. "God, my Angel," he muttered huskily. "Dear God, you're so lovely."

Amanda shivered and drew away, feeling a sudden and irrational reluctance to have him kiss her. "Let's not start something we don't have time to finish, Edward," she said lightly. "You have to hurry or you'll miss your flight."

Hurt and surprise flickered briefly in his eyes but his voice was calm when he answered. "You're right, my love. I'll call you later, shall I?"

"I'll be looking forward to it," Amanda said. "You can tell me all about the new lines," she added wistfully. "I really wish I were going with you, Edward. You know I do. It's just that..."

He nodded, cutting off her halting explanation, and got out to walk her into the lobby, then kissed her casually on the cheek and hurried back to his car.

Amanda stood by the paneled front doors watching him drive away, waving sadly into the darkness like an abandoned child. Finally she entered the elevator and got off listlessly at her floor, fitting the key into the lock and letting herself into an apartment that seemed unbearably lonely and cold in its stark graceful symmetry.

She walked across the kitchen and paused, looking around unhappily, torn by a host of conflicting emotions. With sudden painful intensity Amanda contrasted her home with the cluttered warmth of Brock's.

She stood gazing fixedly at the telephone, thinking about the empty day that stretched ahead of her tomorrow. Finally she crossed the room, flipped through the telephone book and dialed his number, then stood waiting tensely as the phone rang, fighting herself to keep from hanging up.

She heard Brock's warm deep voice, almost drowned out by a noisy storm of barking.

"My goodness," Amanda said, laughing, feeling better almost immediately. "Is that Alvin? What on earth is wrong with him?"

"He was hiding in the broom closet, eating my baseball glove. I just caught him and took it away."

"Do you play baseball?" Amanda said, her heart still singing with a kind of absurd happiness that she couldn't begin to understand.

"Just about the best third-base man in the Claro County men's fastball league."

"I see. That's very impressive," Amanda said solemnly.

"Don't make fun, girl. That's a very tough league."

"I'm sure it is. Brock..."

"Yeah?"

"I seem to have a free day tomorrow, after all, and I don't really feel like staying in the city. Do you think it would be all right if I came out and looked around your house a little more?"

"All *right?*" he asked in disbelief. "That'd be great, Amanda. Just wonderful."

"Good," she said shyly, touched by the unmistakable happiness in his voice. "I'd like to bring some drafting paper and do some sketches, floor plans of kitchen arrangements, that sort of thing, if you don't mind?"

"I can't think of anything I'd like more. I sure do need the help, Amanda. And I'll keep that promise I made."

"Good. In the morning, then? Is ten o'clock all right with you?"

"Sure. Alvin knows it's you on the phone," Brock reported, his voice warm with laughter. "He's lying here on his back, licking the cord."

Amanda laughed and hung up, hurrying into her bedroom, shrugging out of her coat as she ran. Her face was alight with happiness, and she was humming as she turned back the covers on her bed, then went into the kitchen to make herself a mug of hot chocolate.

"YOU KNOW, I don't think I've ever tasted beef stew this delicious," Amanda said cheerfully a few days later, putting her granny glasses back on and frowning at the kitchen floor plan she was sketching onto graph paper. "Brock, do you think we could find room for a pantry here in the corner if we cut down the size of the cabinet by the fridge?"

Brock wiped his hands on a red gingham towel and moved over to look down at her sketch. "Sure," he said after a moment's thoughtful consideration. "That's a real good idea, Amanda. I could even build one of those round things in it, you know, the things that turn?" He whirled his hand in the air.

Amanda smiled, setting down her ruler and spooning up the last of the thick dark gravy. "A lazy Susan," she told him.

"Yeah, that's right." Brock grinned at her. "So you like my stew?"

"It's wonderful. I'm so full I can hardly move."

"You and Alvin," Brock said, indicating the lump who lounged in sated bliss at Amanda's feet. Alvin's round belly protruded alarmingly, his eyes were half-closed and his ears twitched with drowsy contentment.

Amanda smiled up at Brock over her gold-framed glasses, then bent to pat the sleepy dog. "Alvin and I just happen to enjoy our meals," she said. "There's nothing wrong with that."

"Yeah," Brock said with a grin, lifting plates from the table and carrying them to the sink. "It'll sure be nice to have a built-in dishwasher," he said wistfully. "I can hardly wait. I'm buying the lumber this week and starting those cabinets right away."

"When will you be done?" Amanda felt a sudden chill.

Brock frowned. "Well, it's not a real busy time right now. The calves are sold, the bulls are in and the feeder stock is still out on grass, so I should be able to work pretty steady. It's awful slow work, making cabinets. But I think I can probably have it all done, even the windows, by the end of next month."

Amanda toyed with her pencil and drew a few more lines of shading into the walls on her blueprint. "I wonder if I'll still be here," she said. "I'd love to see how it turns out."

He paused by the sink and looked at her sharply. "Are you going away, Amanda?"

She nodded, removing her glasses and looking directly at him. "I'm going back to New York. Edward's offered me the most wonderful job, and I think I'm going to accept."

"What about your business?"

Amanda shrugged and gripped her pencil in nervous fingers. "It's been so hard, trying to get this business going. I'm really getting tired of it. And it's so...so *scary* all the time. You know what I mean?"

"Life is scary, Amanda," Brock said quietly, running hot water over the dishes stacked in the sink. "I thought your business was picking up lately," he added, his voice casual.

"It is. But it's still so insecure, and this job of Edward's is just terrific. I'd be traveling, seeing the world, meeting exciting famous people, having all kinds of responsibility...."

"And living with him again?" Brock asked in the same offhand tone.

"I lived with him for four years," Amanda said calmly. "He's familiar to me, Brock. We know each other well, and he feels so...safe."

"Well, safety is important, I guess. Especially nowadays. I think I'll just leave these dishes to soak," Brock added abruptly. "I have to drive out and start the pump on the windmill, Amanda. Want to ride along?"

"Is it far?"

"Just a mile or so up the pasture," Brock said.

"All right. Is Alvin coming?"

At the mention of his name, Alvin lifted his head and opened one eye, then sighed and dropped his muzzle heavily back onto the rug.

"I think Alvin needs to spend a little more time sleeping off his lunch," Brock said with an attempt at a smile. "Come on, Amanda. You probably won't need your jacket. The sun's real warm today."

Amanda followed him outside and climbed into the big truck, sniffing pleasurably at the mingled scents of hay, sagebrush and damp earth that drifted in through the open window.

"I can't believe how quickly everything dried up after that heavy rain," she said, gazing out at the rolling autumn fields as they bumped along a pasture track leading up a hillside covered with tangled mesquite.

"It doesn't take long. This limestone's so porous. Seems like my whole ranch is just one big sponge, sucking up the rain as soon as it falls."

"It's lovely," Amanda said. "Do you have hired hands, Brock?" she added, looking over at him curiously. "Anybody who works for you?"

"Not this time of year. I usually hire somebody in the spring when things get real busy. Of course, when I follow through on a few more of my plans, enlarge and diversify my operation, I'm definitely going to need full-time help. Look at the view, Amanda," he added. "I like to come up here, just to look around."

Amanda leaned forward, peering at the vista beyond them—a sea of rolling green hills shading to deep blue, then to misty violet, finally lost in the shrouded distant horizon. "Oh, Brock," she breathed in wonder, "look how far you can see!"

"Pretty, isn't it?" he said briefly, stopping the truck on the hilltop and getting out to open her door. "The bulls are down by the windmill," he added, "and that big Brangus can be a mite feisty when he feels like it. I think I'll just leave you up here, and walk down to start the pump."

"Will you...will you be all right?" she asked anxiously, peering down at the largest of the half dozen bulls in the field, a massive black animal who bellowed and pawed ominously near the fence enclosing the windmill.

"Sure," Brock said. "Don't worry, girl, I raised that ol' boy from a baby. He knows better than to mess with me."

Amanda nodded dubiously as Brock reached into the back of the truck and withdrew a couple of soft colorful Navaho saddle blankets, shook them out and spread them on the sun-warmed grass near a stand of oak trees.

"Here, you just relax and enjoy the view," Brock said. "I'll be right back."

She watched as he strode off into the sunlight, his tall lean form surrounded with a nimbus of pure gold that made him shimmer and dance before her eyes.

Amanda's heart was in her mouth when he approached the big angry bull. But Brock paused, made an impatient threatening gesture and moved through the gate into the enclosure, leaving the animal backing up and glaring balefully at him through the rails.

She saw Brock's wide shoulders straining near the windmill, heard the rhythmic hum of a motor and the sudden gush and splash of a stream of water at the big trough. The bulls shoved and crowded around the trough, emitting strangled bellows that started low in their heavy throats and turned into shrieks, then sobbed into trembling silence in the rich autumn sunlight.

Amanda relaxed into the softness of the thick blankets, smiling drowsily at the beauty all around her. Something nagged at her memory, something about this sun-warmed hillside, starred with tiny yellow autumn flowers. There was a familiar feeling to this scene, a sense that she'd been here before, enjoyed moments of overwhelming happiness in a setting just like this.

But she couldn't seem to isolate the memory, and she felt too sleepy to try. She closed her eyes in contentment.

"You look so pretty up on this hilltop, Amanda. Just like a little Texas wildflower."

Amanda opened her eyes at the husky note in Brock's voice. She moved over to make room for him on the blanket. "I don't feel very flowerlike these days," she said. "I feel more like a . . . a weed, or something, Brock. Some poor plant that gets blown all over the place, can't find its proper setting and doesn't really know where or how it should grow."

"Plants should grow where they do the best," Brock told her soberly, leaning up on one elbow and looking down at her with a dark intent glance.

"Where the light and temperature and soil conditions are just right for them."

"What if there isn't any such place?"

"There's a right place for every plant," Brock said firmly. "And every person, if it comes to that. It just takes some looking, that's all."

"And how do you ever know if you've found it?" Amanda waited for his answer, surprised by how anxious she was to hear his reply.

He lay back with his hands laced behind his head and gazed up at the drifting clouds. "I don't know," he said finally. "I guess you just feel right, and your roots start to go down deep and strong, and you grow and bear fruit... that's how you know."

"Do you feel that way? Here on this ranch, do you feel as if you're planted in absolutely the right place?"

"Absolutely," he said. "I feel more at home here than I ever could anywhere else in the world. I really need this place, Amanda. This air and light and these fields around me... I need them to breathe right."

"You're so lucky, you know that?" Amanda rolled her head and looked directly at him as they lay side by side in the sunlight. "It must be wonderful to know you're in just the right place." She paused. "You know, Brock, I don't think I've ever felt that way in my whole life."

"Oh, girl..." Brock reached out a gentle hand to touch her cheek. "My poor sweet girl," he whispered in that same husky voice. "Did you ever think maybe you've been looking for happiness in the wrong place all these years?"

She shivered at his touch and tried to dismiss his words and the tumult of feeling they caused in her heart.

She moved closer, nestling against him, so bereft all at once that she was afraid she might burst into tears if he didn't take her in his arms and hold her.

She felt his body grow tense and start to edge away, heard him murmuring in anguish against her hair. "I can't do this, girl. Don't tempt me like this. I promised I wouldn't touch you again."

Amanda reached over and covered his lips softly with her hand. She leaned up on one elbow, removed her fingers and gazed steadily down into his eyes, then bent to press her mouth to his.

All her repressed passion went into that kiss, all the lonely nights filled with self-doubts and mounting sexual hunger, all the anguish and despair that came from feeling so lost and without focus.

She pressed her body onto his, poured herself into the fiery sweetness of their kiss with a kind of desperate intensity, hardly conscious that her face was wet with tears.

"Sweetheart," Brock whispered haltingly against her mouth. "Oh, sweetheart...you feel so good...."

After another endless, blinding kiss, he unbuttoned her shirt and snapped the catch on her bra, then leaned up to kiss her breasts while she moved above him, her tear-streaked face raised to the sunlight, her eyes closed in helpless ecstasy.

She shuddered at the feel of his hands and lips on her bare flesh, the crispness of his dark hair against her breasts, the gentle pressure as he unzipped her slacks and rolled them down over her hips, then ran his hand under the soft elastic of her panties.

"Tell me," he pleaded in a husky whisper. "Tell me if this isn't what you want, girl. God knows I can't bear to hurt you. You're the most special, wonderful woman in all the world. Tell me what you want."

Lost in the richness of sensation, Amanda heard nothing of his plea except that he considered her to be special and wonderful. For a fleeting moment part of her mind wondered if Edward had ever considered her special, but she couldn't seem to hold on to any thoughts of Edward. There was nothing left in her world but sunshine and caressing breezes and the body of this man who lay with her.

"Don't talk," she whispered urgently into the warm skin of his neck. "Don't talk."

She reached down to flip the buckle on his tooled leather belt and tugged at his zipper, feeling a rising tide of excitement when she encountered his bulge of maleness.

"Oh, wonderful," she murmured shamelessly, lost in desire. "Oh, Brock, please. Please . . ."

But she didn't have to plead with him. Brock, too, had clearly abandoned his reservations and given himself up to sensation, to the tide of feeling that washed and pounded over both of them like a thundering tidal wave.

He stood and stripped off his jeans and shorts rapidly, tossed them away and knelt beside Amanda. "Sweetheart," he whispered, running his hands over her hips and thighs, trailing his fingers across her abdomen and up to her breasts, teasing the nipples and bending to kiss the pulse at her throat, then her lips, her cheeks and earlobes, her eyelids. "I wish you could see yourself now," he murmured against her hair. "I wish you could see how you look here in the sunlight."

She smiled mistily at him and reached out to caress him, drawn by the thrusting hardness of him, aching with need. At her touch he groaned and lowered himself against her. His hand moved down the length of her body and became more purposeful, his fingers feathering against her with a gentle sweet insistence that warmed her, opened her, roused her to an intensity of desire that she was afraid she might not be able to endure.

But he seemed to know when the feelings became unbearable and paused in his tender caresses, moving his hand aside and drawing her into a warm curving embrace, then arching above her and entering her body so gently and with such confident ease that she gasped, stunned by the way he felt inside her, the wonderfully satisfying richness of his body filling and covering her own.

"Brock," she murmured against his throat. "Oh, God, it feels..." She moved slowly beneath him, searching for the words to tell him how she felt.

"What, darling?" he asked, covering her mouth with his own, murmuring against her lips. "What does it feel like?"

"Like heaven. Like nothing I ever... Oh, God..."

And then there were no words, no thoughts, nothing but pounding rich sensation and a soaring flight that carried her so high she was frightened, lost, unsure of where she was being taken or how she would ever find herself again.

A last she felt a shattering wave of pure pleasure, then a throbbing aftermath of fulfillment, of gentle quivering happiness that ebbed through her body in ancient tides, shifting and lapping quietly onto some distant sun-washed shore.

Slowly Amanda returned to herself, became aware of the man who lay silent and content in her arms, of the soft blanket against her bare skin and the leaves rustling overhead, of the distant bellows of the bulls down at their crowded water trough.

She stroked Brock's rich dark hair, but her mind was already troubled as he began to stir and murmur in her arms.

What have I done? Amanda thought, gripping him tightly and staring with blind panic at the cloudless arching sapphire of that calm Texas sky. *Oh, dear God, what have I done?*

CHAPTER NINE

MARY GIBSON MOVED quietly through the visitors' room, looking trim and attractive in a tailored rust-colored jumpsuit that brightened the highlights in her hair. She wore a skillful touch of makeup and dainty gold earrings, and her slim waist was accentuated by a wide belt of tan leather.

Her husband sat at one of the tables waiting for her, gripping a stained coffee mug. When Mary approached the table he stood clumsily and pulled out a chair for her, dropping his hand onto her shoulder in a brief awkward caress before he sank back into his own chair.

"You look so pretty, Mary," he said wistfully. "All them new clothes of yours, they sure do make a world of difference."

Mary smiled at him. "I know. I should have done this years ago, Al. I'm just ashamed that I needed a city girl to come along and teach me how to look after myself."

He nodded, falling silent as the young woman at the next table burst into a noisy storm of tears and her husband dragged his chair around the table, then leaned close to her and whispered urgently in her ear.

Al cleared his throat awkwardly and glanced at his wife across the table. "I guess things back home aren't any better, Mary?" he ventured, echoing her own gloomy thoughts.

Mary looked up at him, trying to smile. "Not much better, Al," she agreed dryly. "In fact, now there's a deadline."

He shifted nervously in his chair. "A deadline?"

"The end of November. Cody says that by the end of November, I have to present him with a financial plan for the next two years. He wants me to show him how I intend to double the income of the ranch, or he'll have to call in the notes."

Al Gibson stared at his wife, aghast. "*Double* the income? Mary, he can't be serious."

"Oh, he's serious, all right," Mary said grimly. "And I can't do it," she added, her voice taking on a note of despair for the first time. "Al, I just can't *do* it. I've been over the damned books a hundred times, tried every way I could think of to cut costs and increase productivity, but unless beef prices go sky-high, it's just not going to be possible."

"Well, then, I guess we have to live with that," Al said gently, taking her hand. "We can just go ahead the way I told you, sell the place an' let you move away, back up to Connecticut."

"I don't know why you're so all-fired anxious for me to move to Connecticut," Mary said, keeping her voice deliberately tart so she wouldn't break down and cry. "Are you that sick of the sight of me, Al, that you need for me to be thousands of miles away?"

He gazed at her, appalled, his eyes suspiciously moist. "God, Mary, don't say things like that," he whispered huskily. "These visits of yours, they mean the whole world to me. You're the sunshine in my sky these days, girl. In fact, it took a while in this place for me to understand what matters, but now I know what I've thrown away an' just what a fool I've been. Wherever you go, Mary, I'm gonna be followin' after you as soon as I can, beggin' you to take me back."

Mary stared at him across the table, unable to hold back the tears any longer. "Oh, Al," she murmured, her heart breaking. "Oh, Al, I don't know what to say."

"Don't say anythin'," he told her, taking a tissue from the pocket of his prison trousers and reaching over to dab clumsily at her cheeks. "Don't say a word. I got no right to talk like that to you, girl, an' I won't do it anymore. You just go ahead an' live your life, an' try to find some happiness. I caused you enough misery for one lifetime."

Mary nodded and swallowed hard, still reluctant to trust her voice but anxious to steer their conversation out of these treacherous personal depths. "About the ranch," she said finally, drawing a sheaf of papers from her handbag. "I brought these balance sheets, Al, and I thought you could go over them with me, see if you can think of anything I've missed that might squeeze a few more dollars out of the place."

He nodded his shaggy graying head and took a pair of reading glasses from the pocket of his blue shirt. With the steel-framed glasses in place he looked older and more vulnerable than ever. Mary's heart began to ache all over again.

"There's no hired help there anymore?" he asked, glancing at her over the rims of the glasses.

Mary shook her head. "A couple of them left right after you . . . went away. And the others I had to let go. I just couldn't pay their wages, Al."

"And young Luke, here—" Al tapped the papers "—he just works for free?"

Mary shifted uncomfortably and felt her cheeks growing warm. "Just for room and board and some pocket money on weekends. He needed a place to live, and I—"

"Vern was up last weekend," Al interrupted, his blue eyes fixed steadily on his wife's face. "He says there's some gossip around town about you an' Luke."

Mary stared, appalled, and felt herself growing even more hot and flustered. "That's just . . . that's just so ridiculous!'' she burst out angrily. ''Luke and me...oh, Al, you *have* to know that there's never been one single—''

. ''It don't matter, Mary,'' he interrupted quietly. ''It don't matter at all. But Vern made me realize how it feels.'' Al gave her a small wintry smile. ''It sure don't feel good, Mary, knowin' people are gossipin' about your wife an' some guy who's twenty-five years younger. An' I guess it didn't feel no better for you, did it? What I did, it was a real terrible thing, Mary. I don't think I even realized until Vern told me that, just how awful it was. But now I do. An' I'm just so sorry.''

Mary brushed at her tears again and reached out to grip his hand, holding it tightly in both her own. Her knuckles whitened with the pressure, and her old wedding ring shone dull gold beneath the harsh fluorescent lights.

THE COUNTRYSIDE swam by, bathed in late-afternoon sunlight that was blurred by Mary's tears. She couldn't seem to get her conversation with Al out of her mind. Or the gentle way they'd passed the time before she left, sitting quietly together in a silence that said more than words.

She couldn't remember the last time they'd shared one of those long eloquent silences, each understanding and accepting the other, knowing without words what the partner was feeling. Mary realized that this deep communion was a feeling she'd missed terribly in recent years.

She gripped the steering wheel and swerved to avoid a raccoon scuttling across the driving lane. Mary brought her little car back under control and drove on, smiling grimly at the irony of her situation.

There'd been a time when she and Al had everything a couple could wish for. The whole community had envied their solid thirty-year marriage, their beautiful daughter and bright happy grandchildren, their big prosperous ranching operation and warm circle of friends.

Now, all that had turned to dust and ashes, crumbling in their hands and blowing away on the wind like a scattered handful of dried flower petals. Yet somehow today a new spark of intimacy had emerged, small and tremulous, incredibly fragile but nonetheless real.

But what could they hope for? Mary thought in despair. They had to sell their ranch, she would have to find another place to live, and what would happen to her husband? Would he join her when he was released from prison, living with her in some small city apartment, walking down to the corner store in the morning to buy milk and pick up a newspaper?

She couldn't imagine her husband in a setting like that. Bubba Gibson, the good ol' boy, the rancher and cowboy and colorful local character, was not a man to be confined to a few rooms in the city.

Mary's gentle face twisted in bitter frustration and she pounded her gloved hand against the wheel.

Why did she feel so guilty? Why had everything somehow fallen to *her,* the need to save the marriage and the ranch and her husband's happiness? Al was the one who'd made the mistakes, been unfaithful, even broken the law in his own wild urge to grab some fleeting image of youth and sexual excitement. So why was Mary left feeling responsible?

Throughout her married life, Mary Gibson had wielded little power of any kind. Her husband had made the decisions, and though they usually discussed the important issues, it was understood that Al's word would ultimately be law. Mary had been coddled, protected, shielded from the harsh realities of life, but she had also learned very little about the workings of the ranch and its financial affairs, and even less about the hidden mysteries of her husband's private mind.

Now, suddenly, everything rested on her shoulders. Mary Gibson was apparently the only person able to make decisions, to take charge and determine the course of events for all the future. Trouble was, she hadn't the faintest idea of how to go about it.

She felt a sudden wistful longing for Amanda, for the young woman's proud independent spirit. Mary knew that Amanda had problems of her own, that sometimes her lovely blue eyes were full of doubts and even fears. Still, Amanda Walker represented a new kind of woman, a person fully able to take charge of her life and make firm decisions all on her own.

I wish she lived closer to me, Mary thought in despair. *I wish I could talk to her more often. Oh God, I wish . . .*

Suddenly Mary's mind began to whirl and her eyes widened in amazement. She braked and lurched to a halt on the grassy shoulder of the road.

In the field beside her, three ostriches ran along the fence line, their heads erect, wide short beaks extended, heavy legs lifting and pumping in a flowing rhythm that seemed elegant and almost ethereal out here on the treed plains of west central Texas.

Mary stared wildly around at the passing cars and trucks, wondering if they saw anything unusual or if she was just imagining the huge birds. But the traffic rolled by at a steady rate while Mary sat alone, staring into the field.

She wasn't imagining them. She couldn't be. They'd even paused now, right beside her car, and were looking over at her with a gentle curiosity, so close that she could see their huge bright eyes, their thick dark eyelashes. The male was richly iridescent, with black and white feathers that glittered in the waning light. His head towered eight feet in the air, proud and arrogant next to the smaller dun-colored females who stood nearby.

The ostrich gazed at Mary for a while longer, then turned, gathered the females and started off at a brisk stiff-kneed walk. Soon they broke into their elegant rocking gallop once more, while the male glanced back over his shoulder at Mary's parked car.

Dry-mouthed and shaking, consumed with a pounding excitement that she couldn't begin to understand, Mary shifted into gear, drove back onto the highway and pulled off at the next exit. She drove up a winding approach road, over a hill and into a dense stand of trees, following the swaying bodies of the three ostriches in the distance.

"WHO'S THAT?" Edward asked, following Amanda's gaze as she smiled and waved at a pair of couples in a corner alcove.

"J. T. McKinney and his wife, she's the pregnant one, and Vern and Carolyn Trent," Amanda said. "Vern's a local realtor, and Carolyn is J. T. McKinney's sister-in-law. At least she used to be, because her sister was J.T.'s first wife, but now he's married to—"

"Spare me," Edward said dryly. "I'll never master all these local intricacies, Angel."

Amanda nodded and smiled automatically at the white-shirted waiter who delivered their meals. Then she returned to her examination of her dinner companion.

She and Edward were dining at the Crystal Creek Country Club after spending a day at the races. In this quiet elegant setting, Edward was at his best, tanned and trim, lounging with easy grace in one of the shining antique chairs. He was dressed casually but still looked impeccable in his pleated corduroys and soft cashmere pullover.

"I do recognize your friend Beverly and her boyfriend," he added, nodding courteously at the slim blond woman who entered and sat at a table near the other two couples, followed by a cheerful young man who grinned boyishly over at Amanda and her escort.

Amanda waved again, then turned back to Edward.

"I should have mentioned that. Carolyn is Beverly's mother," she said. "And her boyfriend, Jeff Harris, is the brother of the man who bought the—"

Edward groaned and clapped a hand to his forehead in mock despair. "*Please,* Angel," he said. "I just can't take it all in. If you must do this, at least introduce me to these people one at a time and let me try to memorize the names."

Amanda nodded, turning her attention to the meal in front of her.

"I *despise* Mexican food," Edward announced, staring gloomily at his plate. "I wish I hadn't let you talk me into this."

"Oh, just eat it," Amanda told him with a sudden impatient edge to her voice. "It's really delicious, Edward," she added, smiling in quick apology for her brusqueness. "The kitchen here is wonderful."

"If you say so."

Amanda struggled to control another irrational surge of annoyance, knowing that she wasn't being fair.

None of her problem was Edward's fault. After all, he hadn't done anything to hurt her or to damage their relationship. He'd just gone off to Dallas on a business trip, secure in the understanding that Amanda wanted to go to New York with him and was happily waiting for him to come back so they could plan their future.

But when he returned, everything had changed. Amanda was preoccupied and uncertain, beset by doubts and unable to make any kind of physical or emotional commitment to her former lover.

In spite of his obvious surprise at this turn of events, Edward had shown admirable patience. He was careful not to push or annoy her. In fact, he was unusually sensitive to Amanda's strange new mood.

Amanda glanced at him critically. Just how much did her behavior matter to him? Did anything really affect him?

What if she told him she'd changed her mind, she wasn't going to New York and didn't even want to see him again? How would he feel? Would he be crushed? Would he cry himself to sleep in the privacy of his hotel room?

Amanda shook her head, trying to imagine Edward shedding tears over her or anybody else.

"What?" he asked.

Amanda looked up at him blankly, about to take another bite of her fajita.

"You're shaking your head. What are you thinking about, Angel? You're such a mystery these days."

"Edward..." Amanda paused, took a sip of water to cool the flame in her throat, then gave him another questioning glance.

"Yes, darling? God, these beans taste awful. When they say 'refried,' they're being quite literal, aren't they? These things are nothing but warmed-up leftovers. Sorry, Angel," he added hastily. "You were about to ask me something?"

"Do you ever cry, Edward? Does anything ever make you cry?"

He gazed at her for a moment in appalled silence. "Well, I should hope not," he said at last. "Why would I allow myself to be in a position where something could reduce me to tears? That wouldn't be too smart, would it, Angel? After all," he added, moving the soft mass of beans to the side of his plate with a grimace, "a man is required to have some strength, isn't he? Society seems to expect it."

Amanda nodded, her mind warming with a sudden memory of Brock Munroe, of his lean naked body and his strong steel-hard arms around her as he lay holding her in the afternoon sunlight. She remembered how his voice had broken as he tried to tell her how she'd made him feel . . .

She shuddered and plunged back into her food, struggling to put a wall of reality between herself and the memories.

Those stolen moments in the sunlight had been the sweetest she'd ever known, absolutely the most exciting and sexually fulfilling experience of her life. But when it was over, when she'd finally managed to pull herself out of Brock's arms, she'd dressed with blind haste and ridden in silence back to her car, grabbed her keys and rushed away from the man with hardly a word or a backward glance.

Amanda hadn't spoken with Brock Munroe since that day, though he called regularly and left messages on her machine. She was still reluctant to deal with what had happened, but she knew that the matter couldn't be put off any longer. Amanda had to question why she had yielded so readily to a passing sexual impulse, and what that yielding said about her relationship with the man who sat across the table from her.

Was her astonishing seduction of Brock Munroe an expression of dissatisfaction with Edward? Or was it just a rebellion against Edward's placid calm, his unruffled composure and self-absorbed ambition? Was she being unwise, committing herself to a man who made her feel so restless and irritated?

But then, maybe the restlessness and irritation sprang from her own reluctance to commit. Maybe when she finally gave in, delivered her life wholly into Edward's hands and let him guide their future, she would no longer be vulnerable to the sexual charm of a man like Brock Munroe.

Amanda shook her head to dispel the thoughts. She smiled wryly, thinking about Mary Gibson, who believed that Amanda was so strong and decisive, such a sterling example of the New Woman.

If she only knew, Amanda thought. If Mary could look inside Amanda's head and see the confusion and bewilderment that crowded there, the lonely misery and the childlike longing for somebody to come along and somehow magically make everything all right...

"You're doing it again," Edward commented.

"Doing what?"

"Shaking your head and grimacing. Could it be that you secretly share my opinion of this food, but real Texans aren't allowed to say such a thing out loud?''

"I love Mexican food,'' Amanda said staunchly. "I'm just . . . I have a lot on my mind, Edward.''

"Well,'' he said mildly, "I hope some of it pertains to me.''

"Oh, yes,'' Amanda told him fervently. "Oh, yes, Edward, you can be sure that you're very much in my thoughts these days.''

"Good,'' he said. "Because we do have some decisions to make, Angel. I'm sure you're aware of that.''

"Oh, I'm aware of it, all right,'' Amanda told him gloomily. "I'm definitely aware that decisions need to be made.''

"That's excellent. So how's this for a beginning, my love?''

He took a sip of water and paused. Amanda glanced up at him, surprised by the sudden crispness in his tone.

"I'm leaving tonight for a couple of days. I have some business in Dallas, Amanda. There was a terrific young designer there who's possibly interested in moving to New York, and I'm going to see if she can be wooed by charm and money.''

"She?'' Amanda echoed, giving him a quick glance.

Edward grinned. "Jealous, Angel?''

"Of course not,'' Amanda said firmly.

"Good. Now, I'll be back here on Sunday to see you before I leave, and then—"

"Leave? You mean after Dallas?"

"I *do* have a business in New York, darling. I can't stay here forever, socializing with all your cowboy friends, no matter how delightful they are."

Amanda shuddered at the words *cowboy friends,* and gripped her napkin tightly in her lap.

"So what I propose is this." Edward paused to sip his wine and gazed at her with the commanding look that always made her heart stand still.

"Yes?"

"Two weeks, Angel," he told her serenely. "I'll give you two weeks after I get back to New York to make your final decision. You'll have to decide within that time how to dispose of your business, when you want to move and just how you intend, generally speaking, to make this transition."

Amanda swallowed hard, her mind a blur of confused thoughts. "Two weeks isn't . . . it's not a very long time, Edward."

"Angel," he said gently, "I have an opening that needs to be filled. I can't wait indefinitely. If you don't want to be my buyer, there are a number of highly qualified people who've already indicated they'd be delighted to take the job."

"I know, Edward," Amanda said in a small voice. "And you're being more than fair with me. I appreciate your patience, I really do. It's just such a big decision. I don't know if two weeks is—''

"Two weeks is all I can give you, dear. I have to have your final decision by then.'' Edward paused, letting his eyes rest on her with significant warmth, reaching across the table to grip her hand. "And I hope you decide to come with me, Angel,'' he whispered. "You have no idea how very much I want you. And how much I need you.''

Amanda gazed at him, wide-eyed, trying to recall if he'd ever said those words to her before.

I need you . . .

His handsome face blurred and shimmered, turned slowly tanned and hard with a humorous lopsided grin and keen dark eyes. Amanda blinked, genuinely wondering if she might be losing her mind.

"Oh, look,'' Edward was saying. "There's your jockey friend.''

Amanda turned and waved at Lynn McKinney, who was walking across the room with Ken Slattery and Nora Jones, heading for Jeff and Beverly's table.

"Pretty little thing, isn't she?'' Edward commented with warm approval. "You'd never think, seeing her in that dress, that she can ride the way she does.''

"She's deceptive, all right.'' Amanda smiled wistfully at the group of them. They were all laughing and happy. Ken, tall and craggy, quietly handsome, had his arm protectively around Nora. He leaned over to whisper something teasing in her ear while the others laughed again.

They all turned toward the main entry, calling and waving. Amanda looked in that direction, too, expecting to see Sam Russell join the group.

Suddenly her heart stood still, then began to thunder in her chest, almost choking her. Her hands shook and her mouth went dry, while Edward glanced at her curiously.

Brock Munroe was striding into the room, smiling a greeting at the group around Beverly's table, his big body lithe and easy in clean jeans and a casual plaid shirt.

"My goodness," Edward murmured. "A real, genuine cowboy. I assume that's the jockey's partner in life?"

Amanda cast her escort a quick distracted glance, barely taking in his words, then turned to gaze once again at Brock, who was now seating himself next to Lynn.

This was the first time she'd seen Brock Munroe since those wondrous moments in the sunshine. But there was no doubt the man had cast some kind of spell on her. She, Amanda Walker, who had always been so dainty and fastidious and sophisticated, was now consumed with a raw hunger for the touch of those large yet so-gentle hands, an aching need to feel his lips on hers.

Amanda felt suddenly, violently jealous of Lynn, who sat beside him, leaning toward him, smiling at something he'd just said....

This is crazy, Amanda told herself. *This is just crazy. Nothing like this has ever happened to me in my whole life....*

Edward, too, was gazing at Brock Munroe in mild fascination. "I didn't know there were still types like that in the world," he commented cheerfully. "Did they make him check his six-guns at the door, d'you suppose, Angel? Is his horse double-parked outside?"

Amanda's cheeks burned in embarrassment. From Edward's sophisticated New York point of view, Brock did seem like a visitor from another planet, a quaint anachronism that had no place in the modern-day world. If she were to tell Edward what had happened, that this cowboy in the blue jeans had been her lover just a few days ago, he would laugh and think she was joking.

Maybe it *was* all just a joke, Amanda told herself frantically. Maybe it was just some cruel cosmic jest of fate, one that she needed to fight with everything at her disposal. And maybe the only way to dispel Brock Munroe's hold over her was to look at him through Edward's eyes.

Suddenly she pushed her chair back with an abrupt decisive gesture and got up, meeting Edward's surprised glance with a small awkward smile. "Excuse me for a moment, Edward," she murmured. "I have to...to talk with some people."

Conscious of his startled gaze resting on her back, Amanda crossed the room with her chin high and her face calm, though her heart pounded so loudly that she was afraid it might be audible.

She murmured a greeting to J.T. McKinney and his wife, and to Vern and Carolyn Trent. Then she paused by the table where the younger couples were seated, her resolve almost vanishing when Brock finally caught sight of her.

His dark eyes flared with emotion, then grew cautious and guarded as she looked away from him, greeting the others with a bright forced smile.

"Hi, Mandy," Beverly said cheerfully. "Why don't y'all come and join us? Are we too crude for Prince Edward's taste?"

"Thanks, but we're almost finished our meal and Edward's leaving for Dallas in a couple of hours," Amanda said. "I just didn't want to miss this opportunity, since you're all together here."

She cleared her throat and hesitated, wondering what on earth she was doing, wishing she could sink through the floor and die, but knowing with desperate unhappiness that this action was completely necessary if she was ever to free her mind of doubts and conflict and make a rational decision.

"Well, nobody should ever miss an opportunity if they can help it," Ken Slattery said quietly, smiling at Amanda in an obvious attempt to set her at ease.

She returned his smile gratefully. "That's right, Ken. And I just wanted to invite all of you over to my place for dinner on Sunday night. Edward is..."

She paused, painfully conscious of Brock's blazing dark eyes that seemed to look into her very soul.

"Edward is leaving on Monday for New York," she said. "Temporarily, at least," she added, when Brock's eyes widened with interest. "And I thought I'd have a little farewell dinner for him. You two," she said to Beverly and Jeff, "and Ken and Nora, and Lynn, you can bring Sam if he's free, and Brock, I'd like you to come, too," she added casually, as if the man was no more than an afterthought.

Ken shook his head regretfully. "Rory has a Little League play-off game in Austin on Sunday," he said. "Nora and me, we'll be tied up all day, Amanda."

"That's too bad." Amanda felt a surge of genuine regret. Ken and Nora were such nice people, although Edward would probably be amused by their casual country speech and manner....

"We can come," Beverly said cheerfully. "Can't we, Jeff?"

"Absolutely." Jeff grinned up at Amanda. "I hear you're a pretty fancy cook."

"I try," Amanda said modestly.

"She *tries*," Beverly echoed, jeering fondly. "Yeah, she tries, all right. Just wait and see. She'll give us baked swordfish with sautéed artichokes, something like that."

"Who did Arty choke?" Jeff inquired solemnly, and Beverly dug him with her elbow, causing another general burst of laughter. Amanda hesitated, torn between an urge to escape and a powerful longing to abandon Edward, sit down with them and join the fun.

But then, she told herself wryly, being torn seemed to be her customary state of mind these days. She was almost getting used to it.

"Sam won't be here," Lynn said. "He's at a dentists' convention in Albuquerque for the whole week. In fact, I'll be baby-sitting on the weekend."

"Can't you come anyway?" Amanda said. "Bring the girls," she added, wondering a little wildly just what this party was going to be like, and what on earth Edward was going to think about them all. Jeff's quirky sense of humor, and Sam Russell's two little girls, and Brock Munroe...

"Will you be able to come, Brock?" she asked, meeting his gaze for the first time, hoping desperately that her cheeks weren't as pink as they felt. "I'd really like for you to be there."

"I'll come," he said briefly, his dark eyes unfathomable, his features calm and composed. "Thanks for asking me, Amanda."

"Is seven o'clock too late for the girls, Lynn?"

"Hardly," Lynn said cheerfully. "Those two are usually still going strong at midnight when I'm altogether wasted."

"Fine, then. I'll see you at my place on Sunday."

Amanda moved back to her own table, still shaken by the enigmatic look in Brock Munroe's dark brown eyes.

But she knew she was doing the right thing. The only way to clear her mind and convince herself of her folly was to put Brock Munroe together with Edward Price in a social setting—and she'd never have another chance to accomplish that feat.

And afterward, when it was all over, Amanda would be cured of this strange haunting obsession. She'd be able to say goodbye to Texas and all the disturbing things that had happened to her since she returned. She could fly back to New York and the life she was meant to live, and there would no longer be a single doubt in her mind, no wistful backward glances.

Not one single doubt, she told herself firmly, sliding in opposite Edward and smiling at him with more warmth than she'd shown since his return from Dallas.

CHAPTER TEN

AMANDA HURRIED around her little kitchen, simultaneously keeping track of the stuffed chicken breasts in the oven, the green beans and almonds rotating in the microwave and a pot of hollandaise sauce bubbling on a burner.

Edward, who loved social occasions like this, stood at the counter with a chef's apron tied around his waist. "Angel..." he said, frowning at the label on a wine bottle.

"Yes?" Amanda threw him a distracted glance and grabbed a spoon. "Edward, can you stir the hollandaise for a minute while I check the potatoes? The damn stuff burns and sticks in a second if you..."

He moved over beside her, dropped a kiss on her flushed cheek and took the spoon, stirring the bubbling golden sauce in a perfunctory fashion.

"I was about to ask," he said mildly, "if you know the sweetness code on the wine. I don't believe I'm familiar with that label."

"It's a Texas wine. I've never tasted it, either, but Cynthia says it's nice with poultry."

"Cynthia?"

"Cynthia McKinney. The pregnant one."

"Ah, yes." Edward nodded approval. "A most attractive woman. Dresses wonderfully despite her condition."

"Well, of course she does. She's one of my clients," Amanda told him cheerfully, but her smile faded when she saw the sudden guarded look on his face. More and more, it seemed that Edward hated to be reminded of her career.

"You're jealous of my business," Amanda told him, poking a fork into one of the chicken breasts. "Aren't you, Edward?"

"Of course," he said with lofty sarcasm. "After all, you must be doing at *least* one or two percent of what I turn over in a year. How can I possibly endure a threat like that?"

"That's not what I meant. You don't like to see me being successful on my own, because it shows that I could get along without you. Right?"

Edward cast her a quick wary glance, but her face was calm, her blue eyes mild and steady, so he chose an offhand approach. "Let's not start a fight just before the guests arrive, shall we, Angel? Suffice to say that you're altogether wrong about this. I'm proud of your success. I spotted you years ago, and your little business venture just proves that my judgment was impeccable as always.''

Amanda looked at him a moment longer and he gave her an easy smile.

''Now, about the guests,'' he said, ''could we run over this one more time, just to refresh my memory? There's Beverly and Jeff...''

''She's my friend, the one I went to college with. And Jeff's her boyfriend, the brother of the man we met at Kickers who runs the dude ranch.''

''And Lynn's the jockey....''

''J. T. McKinney's daughter, and Beverly's cousin. She'll be bringing a couple of kids with her. They're the daughters of—damn!''

''What?''

''Nothing. I touched the oven rack with my arm, but I don't think I burned it badly.'' Amanda rubbed her arm with an awkward motion, relieved that the conversation had been diverted.

Edward still believed that Brock Munroe and Lynn McKinney were a couple, and Amanda didn't seem able, somehow, to tell him the truth.

If she told Edward that Lynn was actually engaged to Sam Russell and the two little girls were Sam's daughters, then how could she explain Brock's presence at this dinner party? Just a stray man who'd happened to be at the table when she issued the invitations?

Amanda shook her head and burrowed in the fridge for her carefully wrapped salad greens.

Edward was too shrewd to accept an explanation like that. And despite her brave resolve to examine this whole situation honestly, Amanda wasn't at all sure that she could bear to have him suspect that there was something between Amanda and the disheveled young rancher.

She paused with the salad in her hands, frowning, wondering what Edward would do if she simply told him that she and Brock had made love.

Would he be angry? Would he storm out of her life in a towering rage?

Not likely, Amanda decided. Edward would be more likely to jeer at Brock, make fun of Amanda's taste, sulk for a few days and finally forgive her this embarrassing little indiscretion. But he'd also be careful to remind her of it every now and then when he needed to regain the upper hand. That was Edward's way of dealing with things, and it was powerfully effective.

Her mind was still whirling with these thoughts, her hands automatically chopping salad ingredients, when the doorbell rang. Edward hurried to answer, shedding his apron and straightening his hair with a deliberate motion.

Amanda's heart began to thunder again. Her fingers shook, scattering bits of lettuce over the counter. She bit her lip and moaned silently, wondering if she'd been a fool to set this whole thing in motion, and how she was ever going to survive the awkwardness of the evening?

"Hello, hello," Edward was saying heartily, always the gracious host no matter what his private thoughts might be. "I see you've all arrived together, so we can open the wine immediately. My goodness," he added in a less artificial tone, "what is *that?*"

Still trembling with emotion, Amanda turned to peer at the crowd in the doorway and saw a small red-haired child standing close to Edward, holding something bulky in her arms.

"It's my hamster cage," Sandy Russell said solemnly to Edward. "His name's Buttons. He isn't feeling good tonight, so Lynn said I could bring him."

"Not feeling good?" Edward asked, peering nervously at the plump furry object in the cage. "Do you...do you have any idea what might be troubling him?"

"Brock says he needs a girlfriend," Sandy reported, gazing up at the handsome man in the silk shirt who had just answered the door. "He says it's time for him to have a mate."

"Brock should know," Beverly said cheerfully, handing her jacket to Edward. "After all, the man's an expert on livestock."

"If not girlfriends," Jeff added with a grin, ambling into the apartment behind Beverly and looking around with interest.

"All this abuse and I haven't even taken my coat off yet," a deep voice complained mildly from the vestibule, setting Amanda's heart pounding once again. She smiled automatically at Lynn and Allie Russell, Sandy's older sister, then hurried back to the counter to continue chopping green peppers.

"Hello, Amanda," Brock said, so close to her that she almost cut herself with the sharp knife. "I brought some wine."

Amanda glanced up at him, speechless. She was frightened suddenly... terrified of this man, of his strange physical power over her, of what had happened between them. How easily, with just a couple of words, he would be able to use that one incident to destroy her relationship with Edward and quite possibly her entire future.

But he said nothing, just smiled down at her with the casual ease of an old friend and set his brown-wrapped bottle on the counter.

Edward lifted it, removed the wrapping and gave the label a quick disparaging glance. "Not quite the thing for poultry, I'm afraid," he announced, shoving the bottle carelessly back into a corner. "Angel, do we have something we can give these children to drink?"

"There's juice in the fridge," Amanda said in a distracted tone, turning back to her salad. "And Edward, if you could just..."

She glanced up in astonishment at Brock, who had lifted a spoon and was stirring the hollandaise sauce. "This stuff burns real easy," he told her with a cheerful smile. "You gotta be careful with it."

"I know. Thanks, Brock," she added, feeling almost faint with confusion and distress. She finished tossing the salad and hurried to place it on the dining table so he couldn't see how much her hands were shaking.

"Hey, Amanda, is it okay if Buttons sits here by the lamp? He likes to watch everybody."

"Of course, Sandy. You'd better make sure he's safely tucked away so nobody knocks his cage over, though. Allie, what a pretty outfit," Amanda added with genuine approval.

Allie Russell, aged eleven, smiled modestly and smoothed her black tunic over a pair of bright flowered stirrup pants. "Lynn helped me pick it out," she said.

"Well, the two of you did a great job. Not many young girls can wear black, but it's wonderful on you. Isn't it, Beverly?"

"Too damned wonderful," Beverly agreed gloomily. "This kind of competition makes me feel old, Mandy."

"You're not old, Bev," Jeff told her, dropping an arm around her shoulder and cuddling her fondly. "Just ripely mature."

"Comfortably matronly," Lynn added with a cousinly jeer at the lovely blond woman sitting opposite her.

"God, what a mean group," Beverly complained. "Where's Brock?" she added, looking around.

"The cowboy? He's in the kitchen tending to the hollandaise," Edward said with a sardonic grin, holding a lacquered tray and handling wine goblets around. "Obviously a man of many talents."

Amanda glanced up quickly. Despite the casual tone she recognized a slight edge in Edward's voice and wondered if something had already passed between the two men, or if Edward just sensed that there was more to Brock Munroe's presence here tonight than Amanda had told him.

But when he handed her a wineglass, he smiled into her eyes and gave her a fond pat on the cheek, then leaned forward to kiss her gently. "Everything looks perfect, as usual, Angel," he murmured. "You're such a wonderful hostess."

Amanda flushed at this praise and sagged with relief, resolving to be very careful for the rest of the evening not to rouse Edward's suspicions.

Accordingly, she seated Edward at the far end of the table with Jeff and Beverly, hoping he'd be fully absorbed in their cheerful witty conversation. Lynn and Brock were opposite each other halfway down, and the two children sat closest to Amanda who was at the end near the kitchen.

"Better put them one on each side so they won't fight," Lynn suggested, earning a scowl from Allie who was feeling very grown-up and pleased by the sophisticated dinner party.

At least Amanda didn't need to worry about the success of her party or her meal. Talk and laughter flowed freely around the table, and even Edward seemed to unbend and enjoy himself, to chuckle at Beverly's stories and express genuine interest in the life and customs of the Hill Country.

The sculpted chrome light fixture gleamed coldly on his shining hair, highlighting the soft rust-colored silk shirt he wore and the rings on his manicured hands. Amanda glanced at him from time to time, impressed all over again by his handsome patrician face and flawless manners, his beautiful flowing auburn hair and flashing smile.

Next to Edward, Brock Munroe looked sun-browned and rugged, almost graceless in his hard masculinity. He ate steadily, complimented Amanda with evident sincerity on the delicious meal, questioned Edward briefly about his job, and spent the rest of the time in a quiet earnest conversation with little Sandy Russell who was seated next to him.

Amanda strained to listen, but could only determine that they appeared to be discussing various types of veterinary problems, including sore eyes on turtles and cats suffering from fur balls.

This had been such a good idea, she thought, congratulating herself. The dinner was progressing flawlessly, everybody was having a good time, and best of all, her plan was working.

Brock's not the man for me, Amanda told herself firmly. *Not at all. Look at him beside Edward. How could I ever have thought...*

But when Brock looked up, intercepting her glance, meeting her eyes, she understood what had drawn her so forcefully. For a brief crazy time she stared at him, openmouthed and breathless. The guests faded, Edward vanished, the room swam in dizzy circles and all she could think of was her longing to feel those arms around her again, those lips seeking hungrily on her own, that hard-muscled flesh burning and thrusting against her naked body....

Shaken and trembling, Amanda looked down quickly and felt a warm flush mounting her cheeks. She picked at her food, trying to concentrate on something Allie was telling her about music lessons, wondering for the thousandth time just what this man's strange appeal actually was.

"Say, Amanda," Brock said, looking over at his hostess again, "have you seen Mary lately?"

"Mary?" she asked vaguely. She sipped her wine and struggled to compose herself. "Oh, you mean

Mary Gibson. No, I haven't been there for a week or so. Why?''

"Anybody else talked to her lately?" Brock asked, glancing at Lynn and Beverly.

"Mary?" Beverly asked. "I saw her in the library yesterday. She looked just fine, Brock."

"Why?" Lynn asked, looking concerned. "What's the matter, Brock? Are you worried about Mary?"

"A little," he confessed. "There's something going on over at the Gibson place," he added reluctantly. "Something real strange."

"Strange?" Beverly leaned forward, her lips parted eagerly. "Like what, Brock? Anything to do with Luke Harte?"

Brock waved his hand in an abrupt angry gesture. "That stuff about Luke, it's all just stupid damn talk," he said scornfully. "No truth to it at all. What I'm talking about," he added, "is all this coming and going. The past few days I've seen Cody Hendricks heading out there two or three times, and surveyors up on the hill by my place.... It just seems real strange."

"I know she's been talking to Vern about selling the place," Beverly volunteered. "Asking him what kind of price they could expect and how long it would take to sell, all that sort of thing. Maybe she's sold the ranch and that's why she's got the bank and the survey people out there."

Brock considered this. "God, I hope not," he said finally, his voice softening with emotion. "Poor ol' Bubba, he'll just die if he can't ever come home again."

"Poor ol' Bubba should have thought of that before he started killing his horses," Lynn said coldly.

"Women," Edward said, exchanging a cheerful glance with Jeff and Brock. "They're so terribly harsh in their judgments. Have you fellows ever noticed that?"

"Frequently," Brock said without humor. He turned to Amanda. "Maybe before you go away for good, Amanda, you should drop around and see what you can find out about Mary's situation," he suggested quietly. "She seems able to confide in you. See if she'll tell you what's going on, and if there's any way the rest of us can help."

"Why don't you ask her yourself, Brock?" Beverly suggested. "After all, y'all have been neighbors since forever. Why don't you just go on over there yourself and ask Mary what's happening, and if there's anything you can do?"

"I did. Just yesterday," Brock confessed, looking troubled.

"And?"

"And she laughed at me. She told me just to mind my own business and that I'd find out everything in good time."

The women smiled at one another, picturing timid little Mary Gibson saying that to her large neighbor.

"Good for Mary," Lynn said firmly. "You might as well just do what she says, Brock. More coffee down here, anyone?"

Beverly and Jeff both held out their cups but Brock folded his napkin and pushed back his chair, smiling politely at his host and hostess.

"None for me, thanks. I have to get home. Amanda, it was a wonderful meal. Thanks again for inviting me. Nice to meet you, Edward."

Amanda gazed up at him, wide-eyed and silent, while Jeff looked unhappy. "You leaving so soon, Brock?" he asked. "The evening's young."

"I'm like Sandy," Brock said with a faint grin, dropping his hand onto the child's shining carroty hair. "I've got a sick animal at home, too, but mine was a little too big to bring along to the dinner party. I'd better get home and check on him."

"What animal?" Lynn asked with interest.

"One of my little Brangus bull calves," Brock told her. "Back a few weeks ago, the day Vern and Carolyn got married, in fact, I pulled a whole lot of porcupine quills out of his nose, thought I made a clean job of it but the flesh got infected. I've given him a few good doses of penicillin over the past few days, so if he's no better by the time I get home I guess I'd better call Manny over."

Edward grimaced with distaste at Brock's story, but Beverly and Lynn nodded sympathetically.

Edward got courteously to his feet and followed Brock to the door with Amanda at his side. In the vestibule Brock slipped into his leather jacket while Edward hesitated, looking confused.

"But isn't... Will Lynn be staying?" he asked Amanda. "Are Beverly and Jeff going to take her and the girls home?"

"Well, I hope so," Brock said cheerfully when Amanda didn't answer. "Beverly and Jeff brought them, after all. We all arrived at exactly the same time," he told Amanda casually. "Kind of a coincidence, actually. I pulled up to the curb and parked right behind them."

Edward gazed at the tall tanned man with the rumpled dark hair, then turned his eyes to Amanda, who felt a sudden frightening little chill. "But, Angel, didn't you tell me—"

"Never mind, Edward," Amanda said hastily. "I think you must have misunderstood."

"Misunderstood what?" Brock asked, hesitating with his hand on the doorknob. He cast a questioning glance from one face to the other. "Amanda?"

Edward frowned, clearly unaware of Amanda's discomfort. "I'm sure that Amanda told me you and Lynn were a couple," he confessed with a charming smile. "How awkward of me. I've been assuming something all evening that was obviously incorrect.''

"Amanda told you that?" Brock said slowly, his dark intent gaze resting thoughtfully on the other man. "I see."

Those blazing dark eyes shifted abruptly to Amanda. She trembled at the force of his gaze but seemed powerless to look away. Standing there gazing helplessly into Brock Munroe's eyes, she saw the truth, realized that he understood what she'd done.

He knew why he'd been invited here, exactly what her purpose had been, that she'd been ashamed of their brief physical intimacy and wanted to discredit him in her own eyes, make him appear awkward and ridiculous so she could dismiss him from her thoughts.

Amanda found herself drowning in a hot wave of shame, deeper and more painful than anything she'd ever known. In Brock's eyes she could see his own pain, his anger and cold contempt.

And worst of all, his pity...

The tall rancher stared at her a moment longer, and turned courteously to Edward, who still seemed puzzled and uncertain. "If Amanda told you that," Brock said in a quiet remote tone that stabbed at her heart, "then she was wrong."

He gave them both a brief wintry smile, nodded at the others and was gone, his shoulders erect, his lean body lithe and self-contained as he swung off down the corridor and out of sight.

RAIN FLOWED against the windows, a cold autumn rain that was silvery gray and bitter in the darkness. Amanda woke suddenly on the morning after her dinner party and lay gazing at the square of blackness beyond the drapes.

Slowly her dream faded, the sweet gentle dream of a sunny green hillside starred with flowers and a baby in her arms. The dream had been as wonderful as always, but today, waking was different.

This morning, finally, after a lifetime of doubt and confusion, Amanda Walker recognized that hillside.

The green flowery place in her dream was the same one where she'd lain in Brock Munroe's arms. The baby in her arms was his child, and it was Brock himself who stood smiling nearby, the man she loved more than all the world.

Now that the truth had dawned in her mind, it seemed so obvious that she wondered how she could have missed it for so long.

"Oh, God, what a fool I am," Amanda whispered aloud. "What a blind stupid fool." She moaned softly, clutching one of the pillows close to her body, trying to relieve the pain that stabbed at her.

Of course she loved him.

She'd loved him the minute she saw him in his poorly fitting suit, with his lopsided grin and the disheveled dark hair. She'd thrilled to the very first touch of his hand, been intrigued and insulted when he quoted the biting line of poetry, struggled afterward without success to put him out of her mind.

And later when they finally went out for dinner she'd been so surprised by the easy flow of their conversation, the way they laughed together, his warm admiration and the comfortable trick he seemed to have of understanding everything she was thinking and feeling.

Why hadn't she recognized those things as the tender beginnings of love? Was she so stupid and shortsighted, so wrapped up in superficiality that she didn't even know the real thing when it tapped her on the shoulder and introduced itself?

Amanda moaned again and rolled over in bed, hiding her face in the soft pillow, aching with misery.

The phone shrilled suddenly, startling her with its harsh strident ring. Her heart began to pound and she heaved herself up on her elbow, reaching for the receiver hesitantly.

"Yes?" she said breathlessly into the receiver.

"Hi, Angel," Edward said, sounding as vigorous and alert as if he already sat at his desk, halfway through a day's business. "This is your wake-up call."

Amanda sagged against the pillows, almost sick with a strange blend of relief and disappointment.

"What time is it?" she asked, peering at the bright red digits on her bedside clock.

"Just after six. You were going to meet me at the airport for breakfast at seven-thirty, remember?"

"I remember. Edward..."

"If you'd let me spend the night," he went on cheerfully, "I could probably have found a *much* more interesting way to wake you up."

Amanda shivered and clutched the receiver so tightly that her knuckles showed white against her skin.

This was another clue that she'd been too stubborn or preoccupied to recognize, the fact that she had no desire at all to sleep with Edward, and hadn't had from the moment he arrived. Even when she invited him to move in, she'd only been motivated by an anxious need to revive what they once had and, perhaps, to use their relationship as a screen that would keep her safe from Brock's unsettling presence.

But she knew now that she didn't want Edward in her bed, ever again. There was only one man she wanted there, only one pair of arms that she needed, one man's embrace that could thrill and satisfy her.

And that was something she'd probably never experience again.

Amanda bit her lip and felt the tears gathering. She struggled to keep herself under control, longing to hang up and give herself over to misery but knowing that Edward would never accept that kind of treatment.

"Why didn't you, Angel?" he was asking her with mild curiosity.

Amanda held the receiver away with a distracted expression, then put it back to her ear. "Sorry, Edward," she said in a small voice. "I must have missed something. Why didn't I what?"

"Why didn't you let me spend the last night with you? I think I deserve the truth, darling. I came down here with an honest proposal, spent the better part of three weeks and wasn't even allowed to touch you. Why not?"

Amanda hesitated. "I just thought . . ." she whispered.

"Don't give me that stuff about not wanting to start something till we got back to New York, or needing to be sure about the future, or anything like that. Angel, where I come from, if a woman loves a man she wants to sleep with him. End of story."

"You're right," Amanda said steadily. "You're absolutely right, Edward."

Of course he was. Even Edward understood the simple basics of human relationships, but Amanda had been so blind . . . so blind and foolish. . . .

"I used to feel that way about you, Edward," she went on. In the midst of her sadness she felt a cleansing flood of relief as she prepared to tell the truth and damn the consequences. "I used to long for you all the time, but it's changed now. I . . . I feel that way about somebody else now."

"It's the cowboy, isn't it?" Edward said, startling her into silence.

"Angel?" he prompted after an awkward moment. "Am I right?"

"How . . . how did you know? I didn't even—"

"I could see the way you looked at him, darling. Your face is very expressive, you know. And he seems like a good enough sort," Edward added, obviously trying to be fair. "If you like them rugged, that is. I don't know if he's the man for you, my Angel, but I suppose you'll find out."

"No," Amanda said.

"No?"

"I won't have a chance to find out, Edward. Not ever."

"Why not?"

"Because he hates me. He thinks I'm shallow and superficial, and he's right."

"No man could hate you, Angel. I think you're being just a tiny bit hard on yourself," Edward said with an attempt at jauntiness. "Would it...would it help if I talked to him?" he added, sounding unusually hesitant all at once.

Amanda swallowed hard, deeply moved by his words. "You'd do that for me?" she whispered. "You'd actually go and try to explain things to him?"

"I want you to be happy," Edward said calmly. "After all, *I* fully intend to be happy regardless of what happens between us."

"Yes, Edward," Amanda said, smiling through her tears. "Yes, I know you will. But there's nothing you can do for me. It's too late. He despises me, and there's nothing anyone can say to change that, I'm afraid."

Edward was silent, obviously unsure what to say.

"Edward, about the job . . ."

"Yes, Angel?"

"I can't take it. You know that. I've got my business started here, and I have to stay and make the best of it."

"I see. But, Angel . . ." he began cautiously.

"Yes?"

"If there truly is no future for this new relationship of yours, wouldn't it be less painful if you were to come back to New York and remove yourself from constant reminders of things, so to speak?"

Amanda considered this. "You could be right," she said slowly. "Edward, you could be right."

"Well, you still have a couple of weeks. You know me, Angel. I'm fully capable of separating my business and personal life. If you want to come to New

York, be my head buyer and my platonic friend, I'll be satisfied with that arrangement. You're still the very best person for the job, whether you sleep with me or not."

"Edward, you're really a good person, you know that? No matter how hard you try to pretend otherwise."

"Don't let it get around," Edward said cheerfully. "I'd hate to spoil my reputation. Besides," he said with a sudden note of pain in his voice that surprised her, "I can't be all that good, or my Angel wouldn't have fallen out of love with me."

"Oh, Edward..." She choked, almost blinded by hot stinging tears. "Edward, love is such a mystery. Who knows why we fall in or out of love? If I could figure it out," she added bitterly, "I'd be a lot smarter and a whole lot happier than I am."

"Wouldn't we all."

Edward was silent for a long eloquent moment while Amanda clutched the receiver, feeling the beginnings of a new sense of loss. In a second they'd hang up and another person would be gone from her life forever, leaving her more alone than she'd ever been....

"I'll release you from that promise to have breakfast with me," he said quietly. "It's a cold dreary morning, my love. Go back to sleep, and sweet dreams. Call me soon."

"Yes, Edward, I will," she whispered. "Have a good trip home."

She hung up and sat gazing at the telephone, then climbed out of bed and wandered across the room to the window. All alone in the bleak stillness, Amanda stood leaning her forehead against the glass, watching the cold rain fall.

CHAPTER ELEVEN

OUT IN THE HALLWAY, one of the ceiling fans needed to be oiled. The mechanism wheezed and clattered on each rotation, echoing down the long silent corridor with a steady dismal rhythm that was unspeakably depressing.

Bubba Gibson lay on his cot with his hands behind his head and stared up at the stained ceiling, wishing somebody would come and do something about the damned fan.

That was one of the worst things about this place, he thought gloomily. You were so helpless to fix anything that troubled you. The only solution was to make a humble request, then wait for the problem to be solved by others who were often too busy or too indifferent to bother. The whole situation was incredibly galling to a man who'd always been self-sufficient, running his own life and business without any help or interference from anybody.

Bubba frowned and rolled his head wearily to gaze at the little white alarm clock on the steel shelf next to his cot.

One o'clock. She'd be here at two-thirty. He sighed, thinking of the desert of time that stretched in front of him, needing to be filled.

These were the hardest days of all, the ones when he knew Mary was coming to visit. He always woke with such a feeling of excitement and anticipation that the day seemed a week long, and every passing hour was increased torture.

And then after she'd come and gone he was so miserably empty and depressed, knowing that it would be a week till the next visit, seven more days of this lonely hell.

He thumbed idly through the pages of a book, wondering what the day was like for all the people he knew, the ones who were out living their lives in the sunlight just as if nothing had happened.

Lovingly, smiling at the mental images, Bubba entertained himself by paging through his memories. He pictured J. T. McKinney riding across the big east pasture at the Double C on a high-stepping sorrel quarter horse whose hide gleamed in the sunlight like a new copper penny. Ken Slattery watching him, and Cal and Tyler, and Pauline was there, too, even though she'd been dead now for... how long?

Bubba frowned, not wanting to think about death, and shifted his thoughts over to the Circle T, where his friend Frank Townsend had once lived. But Frank was dead, too, and Vernon Trent lived there now with Carolyn. Lucky Vern, out on that beautiful ranch with the woman he'd loved all his life, his stocky body full of energy and his brown eyes shining with happiness....

And then there was the Double Bar, Dave Munroe's old tumbledown spread, and young Brock, whom Bubba had known since the boy was wrapped in hospital blankets, as much of a son to him in the early years as anybody had ever been. Brock had never come to visit him in prison, and Bubba knew why. Like any son, Brock was more outraged by Bubba's behavior than most of the community. He remembered the steady measuring look in Brock's dark eyes, the tightness of his jaw the past year when he saw how Mary was being hurt by her husband's behavior.

Bubba moaned softly and again rolled his head restlessly on the hard flat pillow. "I know, Brock," he murmured. "I know, son. I was wrong, and God knows I'm payin' for it. Don't hate me, son. Sometimes a man learns things the hard way."

But Brock's face was still cold and expressionless. Slowly the young rancher's image faded, and Bubba's mind crept over to his own place, to the ranch that he loved almost more than life itself. Tears formed in his eyes as he let himself visualize the big gracious old house, the well-kept buildings, the neat corrals and pastures where he remembered every horse and cow, every corner and knothole and lump of sod.

Nobody would ever know how much Allan Gibson loved his home, how desperately he yearned to hang on to it. What Bubba wanted, with the intense single-minded yearning of a small child, was simply to go home when they let him out of this hell.

But it wasn't possible. The place had to be sold, and Mary was coming today with the papers to be signed. It wasn't even a regular visiting day, but she'd gotten permission from the prison authorities and called him to let him know she was coming. Just yesterday, they'd taken him down the hall to the telephone, the guard standing nearby trying not to seem like he was listening while Mary Gibson told her husband that she had important news about the ranch and was bringing some papers on Thursday for him to sign.

Numbed, Bubba lifted his gnarled hand and gazed at it, flexing the callused fingers that had done so much hard work over the years, that had clutched a young woman's ripe body in a crazy attempt to hold back the advancing years, that had handed over money to have his own beloved horses electrocuted, in another foolish effort to solve financial problems he'd created for himself.

And today, fittingly, those same fingers would hold the pen to sign away his birthright.

Abruptly, Bubba sobbed aloud and jammed his fist against his mouth. He forced his thoughts away from the dreadful present, back into a far-off sunny past when he and Mary were happy, when she loved him and the ranch was prospering and life was good....

Eventually, mercifully, he fell asleep, and didn't wake until he heard the guard's keys jingling cheerfully out in the hallway.

Feeling like a condemned man on the way to the gallows, Bubba trudged behind the guard's bulky uniformed shape, down the hall and into the visiting room that was drearily familiar by now. But this wasn't a regular visiting day. Only two other women were there with Mary, both still waiting for their husbands.

One of the visiting women held a baby in her arms, and Mary stood nearby, smiling as she bent over the blue-wrapped bundle, her face so soft and tender that Bubba felt a swell of emotion almost unbearable in its intensity.

"Hi, Mary," he said huskily when she looked up, still smiling, and moved across the room to sit at the table opposite him.

"Hi, Al. You should see that baby. He's so pretty, only a few weeks old."

Bubba was silent, thinking wearily that the baby's entire life was shorter than the time he'd already spent in this place.

"Al?"

"I get out a year earlier," he said abruptly. "They told me on Monday. I guess my sentence got commuted, something like that, and they're letting me out next July."

"Al!" Mary's face turned pink with happiness, and tears sparkled in her clear hazel eyes. "Oh, Al, that's just so wonderful! Monday?" she added. "You knew on Monday? Why on earth didn't you tell me when I called?"

He shrugged, his face heavy with sadness. "It don't make much difference, Mary," he said. "One year, two years, what difference does it make? Everything's gone anyhow. It don't even really matter whether I live or die, come to think of it."

"Well, if that isn't the stupidest thing I've ever heard you say," Mary told him indignantly. "Just plain *stupid*, Allan Gibson! Don't you ever let me hear you talk that way. It's wonderful that you're getting out a year early," she added in a tart voice, "because I can't stand you lying around here being lazy when there's so much work to be done!"

He felt a little better, enjoying the tongue-lashing. It was good to have Mary stand up to him for a change. She'd always been so shy and withdrawn, so easily hurt that she made him feel bluff and clumsy. But this was a new Mary, able to give as good as she got.

A wave of love for her swept over him, so intense that he felt weak. He looked at her humbly, and then something she'd said penetrated his tired mind, making him sit up a little straighter.

"Work?" he asked. "What work needs to be done, Mary?"

"Oh, God, don't even ask." She shook her head and ran a hand over her freshly styled hair. "I don't know where the work should even start, Al, but it needs to get done, and I guess it will."

She opened a briefcase that lay on the floor beside her, taking out a bundle of legal papers. Bubba recognized a bill of sale, and his heart began to pound miserably.

He looked at his wife, summoning a smile, trying to look cheerful. "Well, I guess this is it. End of the line, hey kid?" he said. "Where do you want my John Henry?"

"Right here," Mary said, pointing at a line near the bottom of the form where she'd already signed.

"Who's buyin'?" Bubba asked, trying hard not to disgrace himself by bursting into tears as he signed his name and gave away the place he loved.

"Jim Sawyer," Mary said, checking the signature. "Here, too, Al," she added, holding out another form. "And here."

He nodded obediently, his mind reeling. "Jim Sawyer! He don't have enough money to buy our ranch, Mary. With all them kids, he can't hardly manage to—"

"Buy our ranch?" Mary gazed at her husband in disbelief. "Jim's not buying our ranch, Al."

"But...but Mary, all them papers..." Bubba waved a helpless hand at the mass of legal forms.

Mary smiled and touched his cheek with a gentleness that almost brought the tears to his eyes once more. "Jim's just buying that little piece of our land adjoining his home place. Remember you always told him you'd sell it once the oldest boy got married and they needed to set up another house?"

"Well, yeah. But..." Bubba paused, drowning in confusion, his mind trying hard to grasp what she was saying. "But, Mary, that little piece of land ain't worth more'n...twenty, thirty thousand, at the outside."

"Forty-one," Mary said smugly. "I drove a hard bargain."

"Mary...forty thousand, that's just a drop in the bucket. You done good, but we need a hell of a lot more to buy down the bank notes."

"Well, it's a start," Mary said calmly. "It's enough to float a small operating loan, and together with that, I've got the money I need to start my business."

"You're goin' into business?" Bubba asked faintly, staring at the brisk attractive woman opposite him, wondering how, all these years, he could have overlooked her beauty and intelligence.

"You bet," Mary said calmly. "I sure am."

"Where?"

"Right on our ranch," Mary said in that same matter-of-fact voice. "Cody approves, and he's even given me a whole year to get going and start showing a solid profit. Right now I'm busy mapping out fences and brooder houses, ordering incubators, making up designs for special breeding pens . . ."

"Mary," Bubba interrupted, "what are you talkin' about, girl? What the hell is goin' on?"

Mary Gibson smiled at her husband, her face pink with excitement, her eyes shining. "I'm raising ostriches," she said.

Bubba sank back in his chair and stared.

"It's a wonderful business, Al," she said earnestly. "Better than you could ever imagine. I've spent so much time researching it, talking with this other ostrich breeder I just met, checking out contacts, putting together a proposal that Cody could take to the board meeting. Al, it's just foolproof."

"Ostriches," Bubba whispered, still gazing at his wife with that look of stunned amazement. "Sweet jumpin' catfish, she's raisin' ostriches."

"If you laugh," Mary said calmly, "I'll bash this chair over your head. Now, just listen."

"Ostriches," Bubba said, choking.

Mary gave him a cold warning glance, sat straighter in her chair and opened the briefcase.

"Look at the literature, Al. I had these papers photocopied at the library, but most of what I know I've learned from talking to other breeders. Now, with the capital I've got plus what Cody's advancing me, I can buy a breeding male and two females, and once the laying season starts in December, that'll likely guarantee me no less than five eggs a week. I need to buy the incubators and pay for the special fencing up front, but the..."

The woman obviously wasn't joking. Bubba leaned back in his chair and gazed at her, stunned, his mind reeling. "Mary..." he began faintly.

"Be quiet and let me finish, Al," she said. "Now, a full-grown ostrich weighs about four hundred pounds and the hides sell to leather-makers for close to a thousand dollars each, but that's not the area I'm interested in. The real money lies in raising breeding stock for other ranchers, and that's what I'd like to do. Are you with me so far, Al?"

"Breeding stock," Bubba said obediently. "Not hides."

"Right. An egg incubates for forty-two days, and the chicks are eight or ten inches high when they hatch. They eat pellets and drink water right away. They have to be registered as purebred breeding stock, and then all you do is keep them warm, give them some running room and sell them when they're three months old."

"For how much?" Bubba asked, gathering himself in hand and beginning to feel a stirring of interest.

Mary looked at her husband. "Two and a half thousand dollars," she said quietly.

"Two an' a..." Bubba gasped and fell silent as the implications of what she was saying dawned on him. "For *each chick*?" he asked in disbelief. "An' you're gettin'... five a week, you say?"

Mary nodded, smiling happily. "Isn't it wonderful? And Al, they're just the sweetest birds. A lot of people don't like them but, I... I've always liked ostriches," she finished lamely, her cheeks pink. "I really have."

"An' Cody thinks this is a good idea? He's willin' to back you?"

"He thinks it's terrific. He says more ranchers in the Hill Country will have to develop this kind of flexibility if they want to survive."

"Survive," Bubba whispered. "The ranch can survive, Mary?"

Mary nodded. "We think so. It won't be easy," she added warningly. "Even though there's the potential for really good profits, most of what we make the first few years will just go toward clearing the debts. But after that..."

"It's gonna be a lot of work, Mary."

"I know. That's why I want you to hurry up and get out of here, Al Gibson!"

"Will you have enough help now, though? Will young Luke be able to..."

Mary shifted uncomfortably in the chair and avoided her husband's eyes. "I had to let Luke go," she said quietly, toying with the handle of her brief-case. "I need the bunkhouse for somebody else. Be-sides," Mary added, looking up bravely, "it wasn't right, having him there, Al. People were gossiping, and even though nothing ever happened, I think I liked to…pretend something might, just to get even with you for the way you hurt me, you know?"

Bubba nodded and covered her hand gently. "I know," he said. "Was that on Luke's mind, too?" he asked casually after a brief awkward silence. "Did he think he'd just move in on the ranch an' all, with me outa the way an' you alone?"

"I don't know," Mary said honestly. "Maybe I'd be flattering myself to think that he had any interest in me. Maybe he only wanted a warm place to sleep, or maybe he really wanted to help. Luke Harte's not an easy man to figure out, I know that much."

Bubba nodded, trying not to show his relief that the young drifter was gone from Mary's life. "So," he asked casually, "who's gonna be helpin' you with these ostriches, Mary?"

"That's another wonderful thing," she said, her eyes brightening, the awkwardness disappearing as she leaned forward eagerly. "You remember Rosa Martinez who works for Carolyn at the Circle T?"

"I think so. She's real good with horses? Got into some trouble down at Fort Stockton an' shot a guy for hurtin' her kid?"

"That's right. Well, she has a sister named Maria who's married to a young fellow taking an agriculture course at the university in Austin. They have a little boy about four, and you know what?"

"What?"

"They've worked with ostriches in New Mexico, at a ranch near Carlsbad!" Mary leaned back in triumph, smiling at her husband, who nodded his shaggy head thoughtfully.

"An' they'll live in the bunkhouse?"

Mary nodded happily. "It's so perfect, Al. They know I can't pay much, but he's going to school on an education grant and she has a part-time job at the library in Crystal Creek. In return for the house and some groceries and me baby-sitting while she works, they'll help me with the ostriches, so it works out great for everybody. And he's such a darling," she added, her face softening. "Little Bobby, I mean. It's going to be pure pleasure, having a little one around the place again."

Bubba Gibson stared at his wife and shook his head in wonder. "Mary Gibson, you're one in a million," he said slowly. "You know that? One in a million."

She smiled shyly, her face soft, her eyes gentle. "It feels real good to hear you say that. I . . . I love you, Al."

Bubba swallowed hard, wishing he had a better command of words, wishing he could take her in his arms and let her know how much she meant to him. This quiet courageous woman had given him back his life, his love, his hope for the future...given him more treasures in this one half hour than any man could dream of.

But the guards were moving into the room now, watching as the three women said their halting farewells, waiting to usher them out the door.

Mary turned and peered past a burly uniformed shoulder to smile and wave. Then she was gone, leaving Bubba alone, his mind reeling with crazy images of sunshine and green hillsides and dancing ostriches.

He followed the guard back to his cell, stepping inside with an automatic murmur of thanks. While the guard's departing footsteps echoed down the corridor, Bubba looked around at the drearily familiar walls and the stained ceiling.

But the place didn't seem nearly as oppressive now. Even the noise of the fan out in the hall didn't depress him anymore. It sounded almost jaunty, a cheery little chirping sound like a cricket.

Bubba peered cautiously out into the barred hallway, then sank down beside his cot on creaking knees, burying his face in his coarse gray blanket.

Bubba Gibson hadn't prayed for a long time, hadn't thought much about God for years, in fact. But he tried to pray now. Tears wet his cheeks and burned in his throat as he choked out a halting thanks for all the blessings he didn't deserve, for life and hope, for the promise of light in this bleak darkness, for the sweet rolling acres that meant the world to him and, most of all, for the love of a wonderful woman.

ALVIN CREPT ALONG the side of the truck, cowering at Brock's heels and casting quick furtive glances into the black depths of the barn. He turned with sudden panic, dug in his heels and tried to scale the side of the box, falling back in the dust in a disorderly heap at Brock's feet.

Mary Gibson shifted a pad of paper from her right hand to her left and bent to pat the shivering little dog, gazing down at him in concern.

"What on earth is the matter with him, Brock?"

"He's scared of your big black tomcat," Brock said with a grin. "Come on, Alvin. Up you go."

He hoisted the dog into the box of the truck. The two neighbors watched as Alvin settled himself with an air of arrogant bravado, pausing to gnaw contemptuously at one of his forepaws. From the safety of this new vantage point, he lifted his head and gave a couple of aggressive challenging barks, then dropped his chin heavily onto an old sack and fell asleep.

"What a coward," Mary said, smiling at the ragged dog.

"Yeah," Brock agreed. An awkward silence fell, while Brock poked with the toe of his boot at a bundle of posts and heavy-gauge wire stacked near the fence. "Pretty stout fencing," he ventured.

"Yes," Mary agreed placidly. She watched as her big cat crept silently out of the barn and began to circle the truck, head low, paws daintily extended, yellow eyes blazing.

"You planning to raise buffalo or something, Mary?" Brock inquired mildly, unaware of the tomcat's stealthy approach.

"No," Mary said. "I'm not." She smiled, glancing sideways at the cat, which had flattened itself against a rear tire and was casting a speculative glance up at the truck box.

"Mary. . ."

"Yes, Brock?"

"Mary, what's going on? Is everything okay here? I mean, you're not selling the place or anything like that, are you?"

"No, Brock, I'm not selling. I'm just diversifying, that's all. Isn't that one of your favorite words?"

Brock studied his neighbor thoughtfully. "You'd tell me, wouldn't you, Mary?" he said. "You'd tell me if you needed help or anything? Because I'd do anything I could. You know I would."

"I know, Brock. And very soon you'll know what's happening over here, too, but I want to get things going before I start talking about it. I promise that when I'm ready to discuss my plans, you'll be the first to know."

The tomcat leaped lightly to the edge of the truck box behind Brock, teetered for a moment and then dropped soundlessly inside, crouching in one corner, eyeing the sleeping dog on his bundle of sacking. The cat's tawny eyes glittered and his scarred ears twitched dangerously as he edged forward.

Still oblivious to the small drama being enacted just behind him, Brock leaned back against the truck box and raised his handsome face to the sunlight. "Say, Mary. . ." he began, trying to sound casual.

"Yes?"

"Are you going to the McKinneys' Halloween party on the weekend?"

"I guess so," Mary said, casting another fascinated glance at her cat, which was now sitting next to Brock's sleeping dog. The big animal was as still as a statue, crouching there with uncanny patience, his muscular body tense and contained so that his fierce yellow eyes seemed to be the only living thing about him.

"Kind of strange, isn't it?" Brock commented in that same deliberately offhand way. "I mean, Halloween's been and gone, hasn't it? This is November already."

"I know, but they wanted to have the party when Cal and Serena could be there, and apparently this was the only weekend."

"What a lot of damn fool nonsense. I don't know if I'll go," Brock said gloomily.

Mary chuckled. "For heaven's sake, you sound just as cranky as old Hank Travis."

Brock gave her an abashed grin and kicked at the dust with the toe of his boot. "So," he ventured, "who's going, Mary? Is pretty well everybody going to be there?"

Mary took pity on him and touched his arm with a gesture of motherly compassion. "I think Amanda's gone back to New York, Brock," she said gently. "Beverly told me she was planning to leave this week, and I haven't heard from her, so I guess she's gone. Although," Mary added with a troubled expression, "I'm surprised that she didn't come out to say goodbye to me. We got to be pretty good friends, Amanda and I."

"Yeah, I know. I guess you two were—"

Brock got no further. Suddenly the cat coiled and hissed, slashing the air with wicked claws while Alvin backed into a corner, barking hysterically, his eyes rolling with terror.

Brock shooed the cat away and gathered the shaking little dog into his arms where Alvin huddled and burrowed, trembling in convulsive spasms.

Mary laughed aloud while Brock gave her a rueful grin over Alvin's quivering ears. "Women are so cold," he commented sadly. "No pity at all for a poor sensitive guy and his feelings."

Still laughing, Mary watched as Brock bundled his unhappy dog into the cab of the truck, gave a cheery wave and drove off toward his own ranch. Then she turned away and concentrated happily on the plans she was drawing up for a set of breeding pens.

BROCK DROVE ALONG the dusty back trail toward his own property with Alvin still shivering on the seat beside him. He patted the frightened little dog with absentminded gentleness, thinking about what Mary had just told him.

So Amanda had gone back to New York after all.

Brock had always known she would, once this little adventure was over and she decided to accept the glamorous job and life-style that her New York boyfriend could offer. But he'd always hoped that she'd come and say goodbye before she left, make an effort to explain herself and leave things on a better footing between them.

"I guess I'm just a fool, Alvin," Brock commented sadly to the dog, who gazed up at him with dark suffering eyes. "Taken for a ride by a pretty face, that's all. I wonder if I'm ever gonna learn.

She's not even worth the effort of being this unhappy, dammit.''

But the words didn't satisfy him, didn't help to
ease the ache in his heart.

She'd laughed at him, used him, betrayed him and
tossed him aside like an old garment, but Brock still
couldn't shake the stubborn conviction that during
those sun-spangled moments of wonder amid the
grass and flowers, she'd felt the same things he had.
He'd seen the glow of love on her beautiful face, felt
her curving sweet body melting in his arms and heard
the broken halting whispers of things she didn't even
know she was saying....

Could he possibly have imagined all that? Who
exactly was the real Amanda Walker?

Brock frowned, his mind tugging wearily at this
same question that had haunted him ever since he
met her. He worked back through his memories,
trying to recall all the personalities he'd seen wrapped
up in that one woman.

There was the cool classy fortune-seeker, and the
independent businesswoman whose air of bravado
covered a kind of winsome vulnerability. There was
the delightful companion who ate stew at his table
and helped him draw up plans for his kitchen, and
the friend who expressed such warmth and affection
for Mary Gibson. There was the sweet warm woman
in his arms, giving herself so completely to the joy of
lovemaking.

And finally, there was the hostess at the dinner table, smiling graciously at her suave New York consort and deliberately excluding Brock, treating him as if he were the hired man who'd wandered into the kitchen with manure on his boots.

He groaned aloud, remembering the dreadful awkwardness of that dinner party, and worst of all, Edward's casual statement that Amanda had told him Lynn and Brock were a couple.

How could she have done something like that? How could she have been so quick to deny any relationship with him after they'd lain naked together in the sun and she'd bestowed on him the sweetest gift a woman could give?

"Maybe she does stuff like that all the time, Alvin," Brock muttered aloud, pulling into his ranch yard and parking by the house. "Maybe for these classy New York girls, casual sex is just another form of entertainment."

But even as he spoke the words, he knew he didn't believe them. He couldn't be *that* wrong about a person. Amanda Walker might be shallow and calculating and pretentious, but Brock was certain that she hadn't taken his lovemaking lightly.

Still, she'd certainly shown her true colors the night of the dinner party. Her motivation had been so painfully, embarrassingly clear... to get the poor yokel in the same room with Prince Edward, to prove to herself and the whole world that he had no right to aspire to the hand of the princess.

Actually, Brock told himself grimly, it was just another form of comparison shopping, wasn't it? She even gave the same advice to women in her television commercials. "If you're in doubt, for instance with these two jackets, hold the two items up side by side and you'll note how cheap and ill-fitting this one is...."

The woman had treated him shabbily. She'd teased him, toyed with him, used his body to satisfy some obscure need of her own and then ground him underfoot so firmly that nobody could have any doubts about her feelings.

And then, finally, she'd gone off to her glamorous life in New York without a backward glance or a word of apology.

"So why does it hurt so much, Alvin?" Brock groaned in sudden agony, lifting the little dog out of the truck and setting him on the dusty grass. "Why can't I ever seem to get her off my mind?"

Alvin looked up at his master sadly and licked his hand with unexpected gentleness, then started off at a brisk trot toward the safety of the house. Brock followed, shaking his head, struggling to free himself of haunting images of deep blue eyes and wind-tossed black hair, of warm melting sweetness and a love that filled his whole body and soul.

CHAPTER TWELVE

A HARVEST MOON floated above the line of black-ened hills. The chilly fingers of its light touched each tree and leaf with silver, frosted the tall waving grass, glittered in the eyes of night creatures and turned the slow-flowing river into a broad ribbon of hammered pewter.

At the Double C Ranch, the moon was almost eclipsed by strings of brilliant lights strung across the yard, over the trees fronting the house, around fences and patio railings. Noise and laughter flowed over the quiet landscape, bright bursts of hand-clapping, scraps of country music and loud cheery conversation.

Brock Munroe parked his truck near the barn along with dozens of others, and made his way slowly across the ranch yard toward the lights and gaiety that swirled all around the big pillared ve-randa of the house.

People drifted past him, laughing and waving, clad in a bewildering array of costumes. There were pi-rates and hoboes, Trekkies and princesses, goblins and androids, all sipping punch and exchanging jests, laughing and dancing in the moonlight.

"Hi, Brock," a cheerful voice said nearby. Brock turned to see a handsome sun-browned face and a tall muscular body incongruously attired in lederhosen, embroidered shirt and Alpine hat.

"Hi, Jeff," he said, chuckling. "Who are you supposed to be? Pinocchio?"

"We're Hansel and Gretel," Jeff Harris said with an abashed grin. "You should see Bev. She's wearing this little peasant-girl dress and pigtails, looks like a million dollars."

Brock refrained from comment, but began to feel a lot less ridiculous in his own outfit. He wore furry angora chaps, long curving spurs with huge rowels, a battered leather vest and a big old-fashioned ten-gallon sombrero. A pair of six-guns hung low on his hips, and the bandanna around his neck rested at his throat, ready to be pulled into position as soon as he neared the house.

"I'm an old-time bank robber," he explained when Jeff eyed him curiously. "Stick 'em up, kid."

Jeff chuckled and turned to greet his brother Scott, who wandered by with his wife, Valerie. Brock gazed at the two of them, admiring their costumes.

The pair from the Hole in the Wall were dressed as cave people, wearing soft furry animal hides, tall leather moccasins and bone jewelry. Valerie had a fetching ornament of bones and leather worked into her shining hair. Bare-armed and bare-legged, their tall splendid bodies glowed with health and vigor and they smiled warmly as they passed by, clearly in love with each other and the whole world.

"Lucky it's a warm evening," Jeff commented, unimpressed, watching as his tall brother strode off toward the house with his arm around Val. "Poor ol' Scott, he'll freeze his buns off in that rig if the weather gets a little nippy."

Brock nodded agreement. "He'll just have to keep dancing, then. I guess I should go say hello to the hostess," he added.

"Better hurry," Jeff advised, peering around in search of his peasant girl. "She looks like she could be rushed to the hospital at any moment."

Brock grinned, moving off toward the house. "Okay. Hi, Gretel," he added as Beverly approached, her dirndl skirt swaying. "There's a weird guy over there in short pants who's looking for you."

He pulled his bandanna into position, tugged his hat down so nothing showed but his eyes and clattered across the veranda and into the house, where more people crowded, their costumes whirling by in a brilliant kaleidoscope of color.

Old Hank Travis was in his chair by the fire, scowling but obviously enjoying himself. Somebody had dressed the old man as a matador, with a squashed black felt hat and a brightly embroidered red silk jacket over his cowboy shirt. Old Hank was well into the spirit of the evening, occasionally hoisting his creaking body out of the rocker and making dramatic passes with his cape while one of the younger men thundered past him with lowered head, pretending to be a fighting bull.

Brock laughed, greeting the old man with warm affection, admiring the indomitable feisty spirit that had carried Hank Travis to the very threshold of his hundredth birthday.

He glanced around and saw Cynthia McKinney standing in the archway, gracious as ever, smiling and chatting with her guests.

What an impressive woman, Brock thought. She was still the perfect hostess, even though she was so massively pregnant that she looked positively dangerous.

With characteristic humor, Cynthia McKinney had dressed herself as a pumpkin for this Halloween party. She wore dark green tights on her slim legs, a round orange globe made of velvet supported on wires and a tight-fitting hood of soft green with a couple of big fabric leaves attached to it. Even her hands were attired in dark green gloves, protruding awkwardly from slits in the curved velvet globe.

Her husband stood next to her in jeans and boots, looking tanned and robust again in spite of his health problems earlier in the year, his craggy face alight with pleasure.

"Good evening, Cynthia. You sure are the prettiest pumpkin I've ever seen. Evening, J.T.," Brock added solemnly. "So, how come you aren't all dressed up, neighbor?"

J.T. peered closely at his guest, then settled back on his heels, grinning. "Well, well, if isn't Bad Brock Munroe, the terrible train robber. The reason I'm not dressed up," he added cheerfully, "is that this woman is set to go into labor at any moment. It's gonna be embarrassing enough delivering a pumpkin to the hospital, without me being dressed up in a goddamn skeleton suit besides."

Brock chuckled and moved on, bumping into Mary Gibson, who paused to give him a big hug. "Hi, Brock," she said cheerfully. "Isn't this a wonderful party?"

"Dammit, everybody recognizes me the second they lay eyes on me," Brock complained from behind his bandanna. "And I thought this was a pretty good disguise."

Mary giggled. "Better not rob any banks, dear. They'd catch you in no time."

Brock smiled, pleased by her obvious happiness. Then he stood back suddenly and gazed at her in astonishment. "Mary...what the hell are *you* supposed to be?"

Mary grinned up at him placidly. She wore a lot of eye makeup and black tights that showed off a pair of very shapely legs. Her head and body were cov-

ered by a long white hooded pullover that bulged
alarmingly over a hump at her small rear, probably
formed by a couple of pillows stuffed beneath the
pullover. Tall feathery plumes were attached to the
hump, and swayed gently in the air currents that
swirled all around the crowded rooms.

"I'm an ostrich," she whispered, giggling breathlessly and standing on tiptoe to kiss Brock's cheek.
Then she was gone, moving through the room with
stately dignity while Brock gazed after her.

He edged his way through the crowd toward the
rear patio where a hardy group was square-dancing
out on the tennis court, cheerfully oblivious to the
crispness of the evening breeze and the enclosing
darkness of the night. The music swelled with steady
primal rhythm, and lights glimmered on faces and
costumes, iridescent and magical against the starry
Texas sky.

Brock lingered in the shadows, smiling, tapping
one of his boots in time to the music with a quick
even beat that set his huge spur rowels jingling.

Jessica Reynolds drifted by, absorbed in the intri-
cate patterns of the dance. Her diaphanous glittering costume made her look like a tall golden
butterfly. She was laughing, swinging on the arm of
Wayne Jackson, who was dressed as Mr. Spock,
complete with tight blue tunic and pointed Vulcan
ears.

Behind Jessica, Lynn McKinney two-stepped to the beat, and whirled down the line of clapping pairs in her Little Red Riding Hood outfit with cape and basket. She was followed by Sam Russell, who made a realistic but amiable-looking wolf in a hairy costume and mask.

Brock's smile faded and he drew farther back into the shadows, feeling a sudden dark flood of loneliness. These young couples looked so happy and so well paired. Watching them, Brock felt painfully alone and unbearably sad.

He stood in the darkness gazing wistfully at the dancers, fighting an urgent desire to escape, go back home to Alvin and his cluttered lonely house, his old chair and books and the solitary life that seemed to be his fate.

He was on the verge of leaving, actually edging toward the back gate, when he paused abruptly and stared, his throat tight, his heart thundering against the heavy old leather vest.

A woman stood in the shadows beneath a trailing fall of vines strung with little pinpoints of light. She was alone, gazing uncertainly into the whirling crowds, her face turned partly away so he could see her profile, the pure sweet curve of her cheek and the lovely long pearl-tinted line of her neck and shoulders.

She wore a shimmering low-cut gown of red silk and old Spanish lace, and her dark hair was pulled sleekly back from her face, gathered and covered with a brief lacy mantilla. Pearls glimmered in her ears and at her throat, and a fan trailed from her long scarlet-tipped fingers.

Brock stared at her, wondering if he could be imagining such a lovely vision. He swallowed hard and forced himself to remember the words he'd said to this woman when she lay wrapped in his arms in the autumn sunlight.

"I've dreamed about you all my life, Amanda...as long as I can remember," he'd whispered huskily. "A woman with a face just like yours, those eyes, that hair and mouth, just like you. But I always pictured you wearing Spanish lace, you know, with your hair pulled back and pearls in your ears...."

Slowly, haltingly, Brock edged through the darkness toward her, keeping himself well back in the shadows where she wouldn't see him. As he drew nearer, he began to feel almost dizzy.

They said she'd gone to New York with her boyfriend, just this past week. Why was she here at a party in Crystal Creek? And why was she wearing the very outfit he'd described in those moments of unbearable tenderness?

Brock's face hardened. He paused, wondering if this was just another obscure taunt, a way of making fun of his dreams and his passion. She certainly seemed capable of such an action, judging by the things she'd already done.

But why bother? Brock thought, his confusion welling up again. Why go to so much effort to embarrass and humiliate a poor cowboy who'd done nothing wrong except fall in love with the wrong woman?

He hesitated close to her shadowy glittering bower, still torn by indecision but feeling the beginning of a deep cold anger. Finally he stepped out and confronted her, gazing into her startled eyes as he slowly pulled the bandanna down to reveal his face.

For what seemed like a lifetime they stood gazing at each other, tense and wordless while the music washed around them and the dancers whirled by in a multicolored blur. At last, unable to bear it, Brock turned on his heel and strode away across the flagged patio, around the darkened bulk of the big house, through the ranch yard toward his truck.

He paused beside the vehicle, bending to unbuckle the big unwieldy spurs when he heard light running footsteps.

"Brock!" she called in the darkness. "Brock, where are you?"

Brock crouched silently in the moonlight, waiting for her to go away. But she was edging along the line of parked vehicles, her steps echoing uncertainly in the darkness. Through the dim gleaming bulk of trucks and cars he could see the moonlight shining faintly on the white lace of her mantilla, glistening on the pure whiteness of her neck and shoulders in the low-cut silken gown.

"Brock?" she said again, stopping beside his truck. Brock stood slowly erect and gazed down at her in silence, the spurs dangling from his hand.

"Hello, Amanda," he said. "I thought you'd gone back to New York."

"I haven't gone anywhere. I wanted to talk to you first," she said, startling him into silence once more. "Brock, I'm so sorry. What I did, it was just terrible. I know you hate me for it, and I deserve that, but I still want the chance to apologize to you."

"What did you do, Amanda?"

She stared at him, her lips quivering. "You know what I did."

"I think we both know. But I want to hear you say it."

"I used you," Amanda said steadily. "I used you physically because I was lonely and confused, and then I betrayed you by using you again to help me make a decision about my life."

"You thought that all you needed to do was put me beside your New York boyfriend so you'd be able to see just what a no-account jerk I was. Then you could leave Texas without any regrets. Wasn't that it, Amanda?"

"Yes," she said, her voice barely audible. "Brock...I know it was awful. But I was so confused by...how I felt about Edward, and the job he's been offering me, and what happened between you and me, and so many things.... I just thought I'd die if I couldn't make some kind of decision and start to get my life sorted out."

"Did it work?" Brock asked her, forcing his voice to retain a mocking lightness that hid the ache in his heart. "Did your little plan help you come to any decisions?"

"Yes," she said quietly.

"Well, good." Brock turned away and reached for his truck door. "It's always nice when a plan works, isn't it?"

"Brock, stop. Please, look at me."

Something in her tone made him pause, take his hand from the door handle and turn to meet her eyes again. "Yeah?"

"Brock, that evening at my house made me realize something I should have known all along, but was too stupid to see. It's too late now, and there's no hope for anything, but I want you to know just the same."

He stared down at her, his anger seeping away, replaced by growing confusion and a dizzying surge of emotion. "Go on," he whispered. "What did you learn, Amanda?"

"That I love you. I loved you the very first time I ever saw you, right here at the Double C after Vern and Carolyn's wedding. I was such a snob," she said, her voice quiet and bitter, while he stood gazing at her in stunned amazement.

"Amanda—"

"Please, don't say anything. Let me finish. I was such a snob that I couldn't even recognize my own feelings, so I just kept thinking you were interesting, irritating, upsetting, all kinds of things. I truly believed my happiness was back in the sophisticated world with Edward and his friends, and that everything that happened between you and me was just a result of some kind of superficial physical attraction, nothing real at all."

She paused to catch her breath, gazing absently at the moonlit pasture.

"But when I saw the two of you together," she went on quietly, "I finally knew how wrong I'd been. I knew that I loved you, and I didn't want Edward's life at all. I wanted to live with you and . . . and Alvin," she added with a sad little smile, "and work and build together and watch things grow. I know it's too late," she said hastily, forestalling him when he tried to speak. "I don't deserve a man like you, Brock. I'm so ashamed of what I did. I just want you to forgive me, and I want you to know that I...I..."

Finally Amanda's composure deserted her. Her voice broke and she turned and ran. She raced across the ranch yard and was swallowed up almost at once in the noisy swirl of party-goers.

Brock stood in the darkness and gazed at the place where she'd disappeared, his face taut with emotion, his dark eyes blazing. He shouted and began to run after her, then paused. His head was spinning, and he needed time to compose himself, to think about all the things he wanted to say to her.

And when he said them, it wasn't going to be in the midst of this laughing crowd of merrymakers. Slowly Brock turned aside and climbed into his truck, pulled out of the moonlit yard full of parked vehicles and started down the road toward his own lonely ranch.

"BUT MARY... why *ostriches?* Why not goats, or... or Holstein cows, or something a little more orthodox?"

Mary turned and smiled at Amanda, who sat beside her on the pile of sturdy fence posts, patting the big black cat named Hannibal.

"Because I happen to like ostriches," Mary said cheerfully. "And I don't like goats."

"But, Mary..." Hannibal arched and butted against Amanda's hand when she paused her rhythmic stroking. He grinned fatuously as she resumed the caress, his yellow eyes narrowed to slits of pleasure.

"Hannibal may look tough, but I guess he needs love like everybody else," Mary observed, leaning over to check on a solemn dark-eyed little boy who sat behind the stack of posts, running a dump truck through the crushed rock of the driveway.

"What's Bobby doing?"

"Building another highway, it looks like," Mary said fondly. "I think he's going to be a civil engineer. He makes the most wonderful bridges out of twigs and bits of wire, anything that's lying around."

"He's certainly well behaved," Amanda said, thinking about how much more pleasant it was to visit Mary now that Luke Harte was gone and Bobby's family was installed in the bunkhouse. She gazed over her shoulder at the child, who looked up with a grave shy smile that tugged painfully at her heart.

"He's wonderful," Mary said. "I just love him. Bobby," she added, "are you hungry? Shall we go into the house for milk and cookies?"

The little dark-haired boy nodded in an abstracted fashion, searching behind him for a rock large enough to prop up a ramp on his highway.

"No rush, I guess," Mary said cheerfully. "About these ostriches," she added, "it's really not as simple as I've been letting on, Amanda. Remember when I told you how I kept dreaming about ostriches, and you said they represented freedom?"

Amanda nodded, moving to scratch Hannibal's scarred ears with a gentle motion while he swooned in ecstasy.

"Well, you were right. I needed freedom from myself and my pain and the awful feelings I had about myself, and that's what this business is going to give me. The minute I saw those ostriches in the field that day, I just knew, somehow, that they were my door to a better life if I could only find the courage to open it and walk through."

"I'm so proud of you," Amanda said warmly. "I think it's wonderful, what you've done for yourself and for this ranch, Mary."

"I owe most of it to you," Mary said, giving her friend a warm smile. "If you hadn't come into my life when you did, walked up and introduced yourself at that party, God knows what would have happened to me."

Amanda stirred awkwardly under Mary's frank gaze.

"I didn't do anything," she protested.

"Sure you did. You made me think about myself, quit wallowing in self-pity and take a good hard look. I had to learn to be my own person, standing on my own two feet, and you helped me do it. I'll always love you for that, Amanda. I just can't ever thank you enough, no matter how hard I try."

Amanda felt tears burning behind her eyes, and fought to control herself. These days she was so soft and easily moved that tears seemed to be ready to flow at a word or even a glance.

"And another thing," Mary went on quietly. "We're going to have to check out the prices on those clothes you sold me, Amanda. I was in such a fog back there that I never even thought about it, but I realize now that I must have cheated you badly. I'm sure I owe you a whole lot more than what I paid."

"How could you cheat me?" Amanda said. "After all, I was the one who made the offer and set the price."

"Yeah, *sure,*" Mary drawled. "And that cream-colored suit is really just worth a hundred dollars, right? Tell the truth, Amanda."

Amanda shifted nervously on her hard makeshift seat, and Mary reached over to pat the younger woman's cheek. "Never mind," she murmured. "You're such a darling. We'll find some way to settle things fairly," she added in a brisker tone. "Just as soon as I start selling my chicks."

"Better not start counting them before they're hatched," Amanda said, trying to sound cheerful.

Mary chuckled. "I know, I know, but it's damned hard not to. All those lovely dollars... Oh, that reminds me," she added, turning to look directly at Amanda.

"Yes?"

"When are you leaving, Amanda? How much longer will you be around?"

Amanda looked down at the big cat to hide the sadness in her eyes. "I'm not leaving, Mary," she said quietly.

"You're not? But didn't Beverly say—"

"I've changed my mind. I...I did some foolish things," Amanda said, flushing painfully, "and I hurt somebody by my own stupidity, and at first I just wanted to run away and leave it all behind. But you know what? You're absolutely right."

"Me?" Mary said blankly. "What do you mean?"

"You're right about women and personal responsibility. Women have to make a stand and be individuals. We can't just run from man to man, begging them to create our lives for us, asking one man to make us happy when things don't work out with another."

Mary nodded thoughtfully, her eyes resting on the glossy head of the little boy, who still played quietly with his truck.

"And that's what I have to do," Amanda said. "I have a business started here that's just beginning to take off and show a profit, and I have to keep at it or I'm going to hate myself even more. I'm not leaving, Mary. I've finally realized that I belong here, and I'm going to stay and make a success of my life. My business life, anyhow," Amanda added with a note of bitterness.

But Mary didn't hear the sudden painful emphasis in her friend's voice. She was laughing, leaning over to hug the younger woman with joyous surprise. "Amanda! That's wonderful news. That's just so great!"

Amanda smiled wanly, touched by Mary's obvious delight.

"Now I can get you to find another clothing item for me. I know exactly what I want, but I don't have the slightest idea where to find it," Mary said, squinting at the diagram she was working on. "God, I've drawn and thrown away dozens of these," she added in a distracted voice. "You just wouldn't believe how hard it is to plan a proper..."

She fell silent, biting her pencil, while Amanda fondled the cat and gazed at the other woman. "Mary," she prompted gently.

"Yes?" Mary looked up, running a hand through her hair and peering at the dimensions of the nearest corral pen.

"You were saying you wanted me to shop for something. What is it?"

"Oh, yes." Mary looked up with an awkward little smile. "I want some lounging pajamas."

"Lounging pajamas?"

Mary nodded, her eyes bright. "Al's got a two-day pass at Christmastime," she said shyly. "He's coming home, and I want to look real glamorous and sexy."

Amanda nodded solemnly. "I see. And you thought a pair of lounging pajamas would be..."

"Something silky," Mary said firmly. "And red, if you can find it. Al's always liked red," she added with a sad smile, "and the colors at that place he's in are so dull and drab. Poor Al, he could use some brightness in his life."

Amanda smiled back at her friend, swallowing hard. "I'll do my best," she promised, her voice suddenly husky. "If I have to scour every retail store and mail order shop in the country, you'll have some red silk lounging pajamas for Christmas. My goodness," she added. "This cat is just insatiable. Don't you ever give him any affection at all?"

Mary smiled at Hannibal, who was rubbing himself sensuously against Amanda's leg, his blunt battle-scarred face glowing with love.

"Hannibal's a pretty tough cat," Mary said. "Not usually the lovey-dovey type. He just recognizes you as an easy mark."

"I see," Amanda said dryly, patting the cat's lean flanks as they heaved and vibrated with noisy bursts of purring.

"Speaking of easy marks, you should see him torment poor little Alvin. He terrorizes that miserable animal."

"Alvin?" Amanda checked her hand abruptly in midstroke, her heart beating fast.

"You know Alvin, don't you? Brock Munroe's ugly little shaggy dog?"

"Yes, I know Alvin." Amanda lowered her face and continued patting the cat.

"They were over here just the other day, and you should have seen Hannibal. It was a scream."

Laughing, Mary told Amanda about Hannibal's stealthy ambush and Alvin's hysterical reaction.

Amanda shivered, imagining Brock's strong brown hands holding the frightened dog, his gentle tanned face and concerned dark eyes.

Oh, God, I love him so much, Amanda thought in agony. *I love him so much that I'm going to die if I can't ever touch him again. And he hates me.... He has every right to hate me....*

She thought about her last sight of him in the cold moonlight where they stood silent and tense, wrapped in their own unhappiness, worlds away from the laughter and lighthearted revelry of the party-goers.

Amanda felt the tears welling up again. She was grateful when Mary set her sketch pad aside and went over to gather the little boy into her arms, giving him a hug and setting him carefully on his feet.

"Come on, Bobby. Your mama and daddy will be back from town soon with that lumber, and we'll all have a whole lot of work to do, so you'd better have your snack now, okay?"

Amanda managed a shaky smile and climbed down from the posts, following them into the house, with Hannibal stalking regally along beside her.

ANOTHER CATALOGUE joined the pile at the edge of Amanda's desk. She sat back, shaking her head, amazed by how hard it was to find a pair of red silk lounging pajamas. With her usual keen instinct for her clients' tastes, Amanda had a perfectly clear picture in her mind of what Mary Gibson wanted. Something bright and rich-looking, not too brief and provocative, possibly even suitable for entertaining holiday guests over a tumbler of eggnog.

But nothing seemed to come close, at least nothing in red silk. Everything was either positively indecent, or else trimmed lavishly with sequins and feathers. And despite Mary's fascination with ostriches, Amanda was fairly certain that her friend didn't really want to wear feathers in the house....

She grinned briefly, then sobered and tapped her pencil against the desk pad, wondering what to do. She could call Mary and try to talk her into another color, but she hated the idea. She hated to disappoint her friend.

Finally, she took off her glasses, picked up the telephone and dialed.

"Hello," she said to the crisp receptionist who answered. "Could I speak to Mr. Price, please?"

"May I tell him who's calling?"

"It's Amanda Walker."

There was a moment's silence before Edward's voice came on the line, sounding cool and amused.

"Angel, you could use the private number, you know. We *are* still friends, I hope."

"I just thought it might be . . . sort of presumptuous," Amanda said, feeling awkward. "Especially since this is a business call."

"I see. What can I do for you?"

She described Mary's request. Edward listened with interest, warming to the topic as he always did when fashion was involved.

"I'll do my best," he promised. "In fact, there's a discount house here in Manhattan that's moving out some high-quality things at fire-sale prices, and I seem to recall there might be something like that in the line."

"Oh, Edward, that would be great," Amanda said warmly. "My client doesn't have a lot of money because she's just starting in business."

"Really? What kind of business?"

Amanda hesitated, contemplating the prospect of explaining to Edward all about Mary Gibson and her ostriches. "Just . . . well, actually it's . . . livestock," she said weakly.

"Well, of course," Edward drawled. "That's what y'all do down there, after all."

"Yes, Edward," she said, smiling. "That's what we do."

"I used it properly, Angel," he said, and she could hear the answering smile in his voice. "Y'all, I mean. I used it just the way you told me."

Again she smiled, thinking that Edward made a much better friend than lover. She wondered how she could ever have been so confused and misguided as to think her future lay with this man, or that she loved him with any kind of passion. Now that Amanda knew what love really felt like, it was inconceivable to her that she might ever experience the same emotion with any man but one, and he was . . .

"Did you notice that bolero jackets are in, Angel?" Edward was saying casually. "Donato just had an entire show featuring them with business suits, evening wear, even slacks. A *very* nice look."

"Really?" Amanda said. "What kind of fabrics, Edward?"

"Very heavy and rich. Damask, brocade, even some chintz for spring. An opulent look."

Amanda felt her interest rise in spite of herself as she pictured the jackets.

"I have one here in front of me, and I was thinking of sending it to you," Edward went on. "It'd be smashing on you, Angel. It's a design in full sequins, black and primary colors with gold braid. You'd look very Spanish and exotic in it. Shall I bundle it up and ship it down? Strictly a gift, for old times' sake?"

Amanda laughed. "Thanks, Edward, but I really don't think so. The way my social life is these days," she said gloomily, "I'd get more use out of a bathrobe and slippers than a sequined evening jacket."

"Poor Angel," Edward said with a distinctly unsympathetic chuckle. "But then," he added cheerfully, "we all make our choices, don't we? I'll call you about the silk pj's," he added. "Ciao, Angel."

She murmured goodbye and hung up, stared into the distance for a moment, then put on her glasses and started paging idly through the catalogues again.

Soon she was absorbed in the fashionable images, remembering what Edward had told her and wondering how she could have overlooked the number of snug cropped jackets appearing in the new collections.

When the little bell rang over the door Amanda hardly heard it. Finally she glanced up, then blinked in confusion. She'd distinctly heard the bell tinkle and the door open and close, even heard the brief patter of cold November rain out on the walkway.

But nobody was there.

Amanda took off her glasses and gazed across her desk at the empty doorway, feeling a rising tide of irritation followed by a cold little shiver of fear. She hoisted herself out of the chair and began to move toward the front of the shop. Then, abruptly, she paused in stunned amazement, her hand covering her mouth.

Alvin sat just inside the doorway, his fat little body tense with anxiety, his dark eyes gazing fearfully at the strangeness all around him.

When he saw Amanda, his look of terror changed to startled adoration. He barked joyously, wriggling all over, then hurtled across the room to throw himself against her legs.

"Alvin," Amanda murmured, sinking back down into her desk chair. She patted the ragged dog, fondling his ears, submitting to a frantic onslaught of licks and caresses. "Oh, Alvin, where did you come from?"

She was laughing, her face wet with tears, her heart singing with a wild sweet joy that she was afraid to analyze.

"Did you drive, Alvin?" she murmured, rubbing the dog's belly as he rolled over and lay gazing up at her with slavish devotion. "Is that how you got here? Did you just get in the truck and drive in here to see me?"

She laughed again at the mental image of Alvin driving the big truck, sitting up importantly behind the wheel with his ears waving....

But she knew how the little dog had gotten here. The thought of it made her shiver, made her glance out at the silent rainy walkway with a kind of breathless tension that was almost more than she could bear.

Meanwhile, with the first joy of the meeting past, Alvin was beginning to recover his composure and think about other priorities. He rolled over and got to his feet, shook himself a couple of times, then began nosing around Amanda's desk drawers and glancing up at her wistfully.

"Are you hungry, Alvin? Did you make that big long trip to the city without a single bite to eat?"

She murmured and fussed over the dog, trying to postpone the moment when she would have to confront Brock. She was afraid of what he would say to her. So afraid...

Alvin sighed heavily and wagged his stumpy tail.

"Oh, my," Amanda murmured, pulling out a drawer and examining the remainder of her lunch. "Alvin, dear, I don't have anything left in here."

Alvin's hopeful expression faded and he began to look so pathetic that she rummaged deeper, digging to the back of the drawer.

"Except for this carton of yogurt," Amanda said, glancing nervously at the door. "I don't know if you like yogurt, Alvin. It's peach-flavored, but..."

Alvin eyed the little plastic carton with mournful skepticism, then indicated with a long-suffering look that it would have to do, since she obviously had nothing better to offer.

Amanda pried off the lid and set down the carton beside her desk. Alvin nosed at it, licked his lips thoughtfully and then dived in with sudden fierce energy, announcing by his wriggling body and vibrating tail that he did indeed like peach-flavored yogurt.

"Well I'll be damned," a deep voice said nearby, making Amanda tremble. "I swear that dog'll eat anything."

Amanda gazed up at the man beside her, the man of her dreams, tall and strong in his jeans and leather jacket, smiling down at her. His head was bare, and raindrops glittered in his dark disheveled hair.

Amanda got slowly to her feet and stared at him, loving everything about him. She loved the way his lopsided grin drove deep creases into his cheeks. She loved the warm crinkles around his dark eyes and the easy relaxed strength of his big body. She loved his hands resting casually against his broad leather belt, and the way his jacket fitted over lean blue-jeaned hips, and the look of his booted feet resting solid and confident on her shining parquet floor.

She wanted to open the door and shout her love to all the world. She wanted to fling herself into his arms, burrow against him and draw his warmth into her body, feel his arms around her and his mouth on hers in a kiss that would last a lifetime.

But she couldn't move, couldn't speak, couldn't do anything but stand rooted to the spot and gaze at him with wide eyes and parted lips.

"I let Alvin come in first," Brock said calmly, his eyes fixed on hers, "because he wanted a few minutes alone with you."

"I...I see," Amanda said, forcing herself to speak, hardly knowing what she said.

"After all, he's in love, the poor little fella," Brock explained with a smile. "And I know how that feels."

"You do?" she whispered.

"Yeah. You see, I'm so much in love with you, Amanda, that I can hardly even remember my own name. So I can sure understand how..."

But he couldn't say anything else because she was in his arms, laughing and crying, kissing him and running her hands over his face, murmuring broken words of happiness, loving the feel of him, the cool rainy scent of shaving cream and leather, the warm tanned skin and the sweet hard lips that pressed on hers.

"Brock," she whispered. "Oh, Brock, darling, I'm so sorry for all the—"

"Don't talk," he murmured, his mouth moving against hers. "Don't talk, woman. How can I kiss you if you keep talking?"

She laughed and gave herself up to his caress again, knowing that it was all right, that everything was resolved between them and there was nothing more to forgive.

Again she had the dreamy sensation of being somewhere else, far from this dark little shop, this drab November day. She was on a hillside starred with flowers, warm and bright with sunlight and a rainbow that slanted across the green hills and ended at her feet, glowing in the mist, spilling golden riches on the man in her arms and the life that lay ahead of them.